ARK

ARK

JULIAN TEPPER

DZANC
BOOKS

5220 Dexter Ann Arbor Rd.
Ann Arbor, MI 48103
www.dzancbooks.org

Designed by Steven Seighman

Library of Congress Cataloging-in-Publication Data

Names: Tepper, Julian, author.
Title: Ark / Julian Tepper.
Description: First edition. | Ann Arbor, MI : Dzanc Books, 2016.
Identifiers: LCCN 2016009531 | ISBN 9781941088296 (hardcover)
Subjects: LCSH: Family-owned business enterprises--Fiction. | Dysfunctional
    families--Fiction. | Domestic fiction. | BISAC: FICTION / Literary.
Classification: LCC PS3620.E67 A89 2016 | DDC 813/.6--dc23
LC record available at https://lccn.loc.gov/2016009531

ISBN: 978-1941088296

First U.S. Edition: September 2016

Printed in the United States of America

10   9   8   7   6   5   4   3   2   1

To my grandfather, Paul

I. LIQUIDATION SALE

Like every day, Ben Arkin woke this morning at 4 a.m. and went into his office, a small room at the back of his Wooster Street loft cluttered with stacks of newspapers and books, and commenced with his routine.

A new journal rested on the antique desk and Ben turned to the first page, spreading his hand over the smooth paper. He reached for an obituary from his obituary file—THOMAS POSNER, FIFTY-THREE, PANCREATIC CANCER—taped the clipping to the journal page, and circled the age with a red marker. After Posner, there was:

> *Newman, forty-two, car accident*
> *Smith, seventy-six, liver failure*
> *Hicks, sixty-one, aneurysm*
> *Vanderbilt, seventy-two, heart attack*
> *Morris, forty-nine, lung cancer*

With each obituary, Ben drew a red loop around the age of the deceased and taped the square of newspaper into the journal. Why, at eighty-three, to see that he had outlived other men gave Ben a good feeling about himself and the day at hand.

Exercise followed. Two sets of ten push-ups, three sets of twelve sit-ups, three sets of eight barbell curls, four sets of ten jumping jacks, one minute of toe touches, five squats. Below the last obit he wrote down his stats. He took pleasure in looking over the numbers. They were proof of effort in his battle against aging. He liked to clear away his long list of enemies and concentrate on the one named aging in particular. Doing this now, he closed his eyes, pressed his hands together before his chest, and hummed aloud a long, deep note.

Moving on, he addressed sleep. Looking at the chart, he saw:

May 1st, 2014 - 7 hours
May 2nd, 2014 - 8.5 hours
May 3rd, 2014 - 7.5 hours
May 4th, 2014 - 8.25 hours
May 5th, 2014 - 7.5 hours

For last night, the sixth of May, Ben, checking his Mickey Mouse watch and doing the math, wrote down eight hours. It pained him to think of all the time he slept away, creating nothing. Yet he knew that his genius depended more than anything on a good night's rest. In fact, on his list of enemies, fatigue directly followed aging. She was a true bitch. But he had methods for fending her off, too. The ten-minute nap was king. Coffee, yes. However, he also liked to run the bristles of a brush along his body, first the palms, then the neck, then the stomach and chest, for this inspired the skin and senses to awaken.

On the next journal page, he listed yesterday's fruit and vegetable consumption, his vitamin intake, as well as the herbs, roots, and powders he had bought in Chinatown and ingested after lunch:

One multivitamin
Two tablespoons of fresh ginger
Handful of goji berries
One stalk of broccoli
Small scoop of cinnamon
One apple

Go to Chinatown, observe the physical toughness of the very oldest Chinese New Yorkers, and soak in that energy. This was Ben's order to himself, and he did it nearly every day for inspiration. In the last year, as well, Ben had begun posting notes around the loft, by the toilet, at the front door. Things like:

Swoop down. Scoop up. Not me. Not yet.
That Pain Is In Your Head.
I Remember.

At the next moment, he prepared a new note, PICASSO DIED YOUNG, and glued it to the door of his office. Then he read yesterday's newspapers, showered, shaved, and drank two cups of strong black coffee.

By 7:30 a.m., he was in the art studio with his assistant, Jerome, wrapping the edges of a blank six-by-four-foot canvas in dress-tie material. Many of the ties were the first ever made by Ralph Lauren, worn by Ben thirty-five years earlier, when he was still an ad man. The artist, in his white robe, his gray fringe standing on end from nervous stroking and blue eyes pulsating, was using a scalpel to open the stitching and then stapling the material to the edge of the canvas. He gave the impression of an escapee from a mental ward, a subway panhandler, one of the down-and-out forgotten. It was a look he had spent years cultivating.

His wife, Eliza Arkin, stood behind him in leopard-print pajamas. Her haircut was a perfect dark red bob. Her earrings were gold and jade. Although her Parkinson's medication worked mornings, there was still the semi-paralysis to combat, and her nurse, Violet, a short, heavy yet strong Jamaican woman, waited in the nearby doorway. Grinding out a pain-free look on her china doll face, Eliza was thinking of how hideous a thing her husband had made. Of course, having heard him complain many times of how the paintings at the Metropolitan Museum of Art were hung in such extravagant frames that you couldn't even see the artwork, Eliza knew what this was about. And it wasn't beauty. This was an act of rebellion. But her husband, at eighty-three, was too old to rebel. At his age, and hers, eighty-one, they should be living in Miami Beach, Collins Avenue, in a simple apartment along the beach with a balcony overlooking the Atlantic, not in this factory.

Granted, it gave her enormous satisfaction to tell anyone how she'd paid only one hundred and sixty-three thousand for her SoHo residence in 1976, and that these days it would fetch six million easily. Yet the envy of those passing below her windows didn't justify the trouble of making a home here. In winter, they froze, the draughts terrible. During summer, they spent five figures on air conditioning. The wood floors had a unique octagonal pattern, but they'd had to replace a panel just last month, and it had cost the same as a pair of round-trip plane tickets to Paris. Pipes ran everywhere—along the walls, across the ceilings, at the backs of closets and the pantry, the laundry room and bathrooms. They could cover them up, but the old pipes would inevitably leak. Then they were cutting into walls, and the bills for reconstruction were astronomical. Worst of all, her husband's art was everywhere. The living room was over two thousand square feet, and there was hardly room for the sofa and television—his paintings and sculptures were packed in, giving her home the feel of a warehouse. Ben rented a warehouse in Jersey City, a six-thousand-square-foot basement space where thousands of his works were stored. And yet, why did he even make any of this art? He had never sold a single piece.

She said to him, "You waste all my money on this nonsense."

Ben snatched another tie from the box, slashing it up the belly, saying nothing. He'd never believed Beethoven's late-life deafness was anything more than wishful thinking brought to fruition. You had to want to tune out the world that badly. Then you might wake one morning to discover your prayers had been answered. Ben tapped one ear and then the other to test his own. They were big ears.

To support his back, the artist wore a brown weightlifter's belt, and beneath the white robe, on top and bottom, were gray sweats. His feet were bare. He stood with his knuckles propped on his ribs, so that his elbows stuck out wide, muttering under his breath. Now he took a pink tie in his hand. In an adjacent box, awaiting his scalpel, were eight suits handmade on the Savile Row. He hadn't put one on in over fourteen years. The occasion had been his fiftieth wedding anniversary. He saw no reason to hold onto any of them. He would never get dressed up again. He draped the tie along the edge of the canvas, readied the staple gun and released:

Pop!

Eliza's thirteen medications gave her dry mouth, and there was the sound of her tongue sticking and unsticking to the insides of her cheeks. She said, "I've made up my mind, Ben. We'll sell some of my diamonds to the Russian. We can go to Forty-Seventh Street tomorrow and speak with him. He gives the best prices for diamonds. It's what we'll do. And I'm comfortable leaving the diamonds with the Russian. The thing is, he's not going to pay up front."

Ben's thumb massaged the dimple in his chin.

"…you have to let him sell the diamonds first," Eliza was saying. "He's very good, though. He'll sell them, and then we'll get the money. Probably next week at the earliest."

"Good," Ben replied.

"But it's okay to give him a little time. We don't need the money today. All the same, tomorrow we'll go to Forty-Seventh Street."

Having already given his answer, Ben wouldn't waste physical or mental energy speaking to the same point twice. Instead, he grunted. A grunt, Ben had concluded long ago, did give the body and spirit a worthy lift.

"Then it's settled," Eliza said. "Tomorrow."

Eliza went to lie on the sofa at the back of the loft. She spent whole days there, watching cable news on the fourteen-inch television, reading fashion and tabloid magazines, dozing in and out of sleep. At the moment, she was thinking of all the money she would get from selling the diamonds. She felt extremely confident. Why shouldn't she? Ask a man to turn shit into gold—it was doable but hardly easy. She would give the Russian great stuff. Her father, Karl Fischer, had only bought her mother, Ruth, the very best. Karl had done so well for himself. His business? Steel file cabinets. He'd locked down the account with the U.S. Armed Services and it had been big money from there out. Ruth would sit with her daughter on the large brass bed—a pile of diamonds, so bright, so pretty, between them—and Eliza would tell her mother how they were the most beautiful things.

"Never say a word of this to your brothers and sisters, but I'm going to give them all to you one day," her mother told her.

An eager young girl, enthralled with the stones, Eliza asked, "When?"

"Right after you marry," her mother replied.

Three years later, Ben did propose to Eliza. She was in love with him. So she thought. A very handsome man, at the time giving full financial support to his mother and three siblings, earning a good salary and clearly on his way to making a heck of a lot more. Yes, both Eliza and her parents felt extremely optimistic about Ben's economic outlook. That said, when Ben first kissed Eliza it was the diamonds that flashed through her mind. Even now, she could recall Ben returning to her lips for a second kiss. A fine kisser, indeed. But she knew the truth of her weakening stomach, her sweaty palms and feet.

Then, on the day after the wedding, while with her mother at the house in Forest Hills, Ruth, who'd had that Old World physique—the tremendous bosom, a full-barreled middle, an elephant's buttocks, and thick rings of flesh for a neck—said to her daughter, "I have a gift for you. Come with me."

In Ruth's bedroom, it was difficult for Eliza to help her mother move the brass bed. Her hands were damp against the metal. Her legs were unstable. But she managed, yes. With the bed set at an angle, Ruth lifted up a piece of the floorboard, reached down, and pulled out a cigar box. She said, "You remember what I promised you, dear?" She flipped open the lid of the cigar box, revealing the stones. "Take any one you like."

Eliza had suffered neuralgia as a child, and, with her fingers massaging her face, she seemed just then to be enduring the painful symptoms of that condition. She said, "Only one?"

Ruth nodded.

"You told me I could have them all."

"Better I give you one a year."

"Why?"

"It will be our special thing."

"But you said I could have them all when I married. That's what you said."

"Eliza."

"Well, it's what you said!"

"Eliza!"

"But you said it! You did!"

"Would you rather I gave you nothing?"

At that, Eliza took command of herself, apologized, and left with a single diamond.

Ruth lived till her early nineties, and their tradition was observed each year. But toward the end of her mother's life, even though Ruth was handing off a stone whose value was high, the ritual of sitting on her mother's bed and choosing her diamond had long felt silly to Eliza. That is to say, it made her feel young, like a child, and for that reason, Eliza told herself, she held little attachment to the diamonds and didn't mind exchanging them for so much cash.

The next morning, the Arkins rode in the Cadillac to the Diamond District. From the passenger seat, Ben punched the end of his cane into the floor of the car and groaned, oblivious to his noise-making and the unhappiness it was causing his wife in the back seat and his assistant, Jerome, behind the wheel. For the third time today, Ben was calculating Jerome's and Violet's wages, the cost of Eliza's medication, the upkeep for the loft and the house in Southampton, the loans against both homes which he had to pay back each month, as well as his art supplies. It all ran him about twenty-five thousand a month. The Arkins only had sixty thousand in the bank. To think there'd once been so much money, many millions. Over the decades, with the sizeable expenses and no earnings, that figure had dwindled. It was true there was much more jewelry, gold and other diamond pieces, perhaps two million dollars' worth. And the houses, yes. Ben wanted to sell Southampton, but he knew it might kill Eliza. He had bought the place in 1981, for her. Leisure meant little to him. A mere hundred yards from the ocean and sand, it was where he did his thinking. Every Saturday and Sunday morning, sitting at the head of the dining table with books, his pile of newspaper clippings, his journals, and a cup of red and black pens, and staying there and *Einsteining it* until 5 p.m. He believed that this practice opened up a side of his brain that made the never-before-seen possible.

Could he execute and dream up his new ideas in New York?

Perhaps he would have to, he reckoned.

Yes, perhaps so.

Two times in the past the Russian had come through on his promise to take, sell, and pay the Arkins for jewelry they'd brought him. His fee was twenty percent. Yet never had the Arkins come with so much. The Russian looked at the diamonds with his clean, square face turned in confusion. They were of an exquisite cut. There were twenty-eight of them. He asked how they'd acquired the stones. Eliza said, "They were my mother's."

"She was a jewel thief?" the dealer asked, his thin eyebrows lifting.

Eliza wasn't amused. "*Nooo.* She married a smart man."

The Russian smiled. "Like her daughter."

Eliza glanced doubtfully at her husband. "Right," she said.

"You must have bought your wife a lot of jewelry, eh?"

Ben puckered his lips. His face resembled a bald eagle's in the scowling eyes, the aquiline nose. "You going to take all day or what?"

Pointing at Ben, his fingers clean, the nails manicured, glossy, the Russian said, "I like you. No bullshit."

The Russian leaned against a long white counter, studying the diamonds with a magnifying glass which he wore like a ring on his finger. His breathing was strong with concentration, and Ben and Eliza swayed ever so slightly with the sound of air coming in and out of the younger man's mouth. Earlier that morning, Eliza had applied red lipstick, but here she wiped away what remained of it, leaving red streaks below her wrinkled bottom lip. Ben's feet were so swollen day in and day out that he couldn't fit them into the kinds of shoes sold in stores. Last month he'd had a pair custom-made. They were very wide brown leather shoes. But he felt now as if his feet required slightly more room. They were constricted, suffocating. Seeing a chair, he thought he might sit down and undo the laces. It was exactly what he needed, yes.

But then the Russian sighed, lowering the magnifying glass away from his eye. Eliza and Ben were, all of a sudden, standing upright with their attention directed right at him. The Russian was saying, "Yes, well, I'll see what I can do. The market is tough. I think I should be able to sell them. Though one never knows."

"They're extremely valuable," Eliza assured him.

At which point, Ben said, "Shut up, Eliza!" He took his wife firmly by the arm, thanking the Russian and leading her out the door.

For the artist and his wife, the following days were especially difficult. Should they call the Russian or wait for him to contact them? Whenever the phone rang, they both perked up, expecting news of the diamonds. A week passed, and another week, and still no word. Eliza was having a hard time sleeping. Ben couldn't work. He cooked instead. He had always been a nervous eater and chef. The kitchen was a place where he could shut out the world. The grocery store, too.

With coupons in hand, he went five blocks through an early summer afternoon drizzle to the Morton Williams on the corner of Bleecker and La Guardia. Crescent rolls were on sale, as were chicken nuggets, lite cola, salt-free potato chips. Ben didn't want any of these products. But it was nearly impossible for him to resist a discounted item. Oh, did he love the grocery store. The food, but also the arrangement of the food. The stocking of milk and juice and eggs and meat and coffee and produce and the jars of tomato sauce and boxes of cereal—there was an aesthetic brilliance here that Ben admired. He was partial to the frozen food section. Take the waffles. The packaging's strong primary colors set against the light and glass of the refrigerator was powerful enough to hold him in place. To mesmerize. To narcotize.

"Just lovely," he said to himself.

He reached into his pocket for a pen, removed the cap, and, on the back of a coupon offering a twenty percent discount on bran flakes, wrote, "There is an idea in refrigeration. Refrigerators. *Einstein it.*"

At home, Ben began preparing a chicken soup. It wouldn't be ready for some time, but he brought plain yogurt and melon in to his wife, who was in bed reading *Vogue*. During late afternoons, Eliza was at her physical worst, with the spastic motion of her arms, legs, and head. It had been this way for years. Ben spoon-fed Eliza. She could hardly sit up. She was having trouble taking in breaths. Seeing her wheeze, Ben proposed driving out to Southampton the next morning. He could have Jerome pick up the car at 6 a.m., they would be on the road shortly thereafter, Eliza would be lying under an umbrella on the beach by 8:30. She would feel better there. Her health, her spirits, always improved when she left the city and came into contact with the ocean air and open sky.

Eliza said, "Yes," though it required much of her.

Ben prepared a second spoonful of yogurt. The anger that lived in his eyes and shaped his mouth and brows vanished the instant Eliza swallowed. Ben liked feeding his wife; it made him feel close to her. Now, dabbing her lips with a tissue, Ben proposed that Violet join them. With her nurse there, Eliza could be pushed in the chair along the beach, as well as have a companion with whom to pass the time.

"Would you like that?" Ben asked.

Eliza said she would. Ben told her that it was settled then. He could use a break from the loft, himself. To get away from New York and refresh his mind. Yes, a few days of reading, and walking, and thinking, and communing with nature, and cooking, and writing in his journal, gardening, and cutting coupons would be excellent for his mental wellbeing.

"I'll try Jerome and Violet now," Ben said, standing from the bed.

But at the next moment, the phone began to ring. Ben reached for the portable, stumbling on empty water glasses and magazines and a vibrating contraption meant for massaging a person, which were littered around the bed. Ben glared at the floor. "Damn it to hell!" Then he screamed into the phone, "What do you want!"

In fact, it was the Russian calling to say the sale of the diamonds had been finalized.

"Yeah? So what?"

The Russian said he didn't talk numbers over the phone. Nevertheless, he was in a kind of frenzy about his triumph.

"A big score," he told Ben. "You can come pick up your money in the morning."

"Who was that?" Eliza asked, once Ben was off.

"It was the Russian," he said. "Seems our horse came in."

A moment later, everything turned. Ben was shaking his hands over his head in a kind of ecstasy. He kissed his wife on the lips. Eliza was suddenly up out of the bed, and, though she used a walker, she was mobile. Ben had a bottle of non-alcoholic red wine in the pantry. He popped the cork and set dinner for himself and his wife at the kitchen counter, a rarity. And that night they slept undisturbed, straight into the morning.

At 10 a.m., Jerome drove Ben and Eliza up to Forty-Seventh Street to see the Russian. In the elevator, the long-married couple didn't glance each other's way. On the fourth floor, there was a single small, square window looking into the Russian's office, a security measure. Eliza rang the buzzer, and in a moment the Russian was staring back at her, his cheerful grin filling the window.

Seeing the diamond dealer, Eliza said, "He's here."

Ben replied, "No shit," and he took his pants up higher on his waist.

The door opened, and, with his head lowered, the Russian stood aside to let Ben and Eliza pass. "Toward the rear," the Russian said.

Ben walked, using the wall for assistance, and was the last among them to take his seat at the round table in the smoky back room. A lit cigarette burned in an ashtray on the windowsill. The Russian stamped it out, reached under the table, and presented a large black backpack, resting it on a metal stool. The backpack appeared full. And though it was the oversized kind used for camping, it surprised Ben and Eliza both to see just a backpack. They'd each imagined a bigger piece of luggage. Perhaps a suitcase. They stared at one another, skeptical. All of a sudden, the Russian was drawing back the zipper. Ben's heart began to thrump. Eliza's, too. She said to him, "How much is it?"

"A lot," said the Russian.

"A lot?" Eliza repeated.

"Yes," the Russian said.

Ben, who'd looked greatly damaged a moment earlier, seemed to come alive. He could sense kindness from the universe. He could feel it between his fingers, which he rubbed together in small circles.

"So what you have here," said the Russian, "is two hundred and eighty thousand dollars. I'm extremely happy. Go ahead and count it, if you like."

There was silence in the room. Then the Russian lit a cigarette. He shook out the match, tossing it in the ashtray.

Ben fell back into his chair. "That's pretty damn good," he said.

To Eliza, it seemed her chest had grown large with pressure, but now that discomfort began to subside. "This is very good," she said.

"Everyone's pleased?" the Russian asked.

"Yes," Ben said.

Eliza released a large breath of air. "Very," she said.

Ben and Eliza gazed at one another again. What they shared wasn't a look of satisfaction, but one that insisted on an immediate departure. Why, who knew what would happen if they stuck around? Armed men could come busting through the door, take their money, and their lives. Any person who'd lived a day knew the extreme danger of staying even another minute. And so, thanking the Russian, Ben and Eliza stood, grabbed the backpack, and left the office at once, hurrying into the Cadillac, where Jerome waited at the wheel.

"You can drive," Ben told his assistant.

Jerome pulled out into the street.

Forty-Seventh between Fifth and Sixth Avenue, the Diamond District, was one of the blocks in the borough of Manhattan that had refused to clean up. The buildings were black with dirt. Up and down the potholed street chintzy neon signs advertised gold and diamonds. Jewelers ripped off men ready to spend on engagement rings. But Ben, in the passenger seat, felt he'd been spared the harshest treatment.

Jerome said, "Ark, you look happy."

Ben's upper lip rose on one side. It wasn't a smile but a snarl. The artist kept caps in the glove compartment, bought them by the dozen at a Salvation Army in Hoboken. The one he pulled over his head promoted an auto body shop in Coxsackie, New York. He handled the brim roughly, bending it in half at the middle. Eliza, in the rear of the car, unzipped the backpack, admiring the stacks of hundred dollar bills. Two hundred and eighty thousand dollars. It was a lot of money. She smiled at her haul, then said to her husband, "You know what...we'll stop for a box of Melba toast on the way home. I'm in the mood for Melba toast."

Forty minutes later, Ben and Eliza were sitting at the kitchen counter eating Melba toast and cottage cheese and yesterday's roast chicken. Eliza was talking about the money. She looked well. Her face had color and her dark eyes were vibrant. The subject seemed to be giving her added strength. She said the bills would be stowed in the safe in their closet. Jerome was the only one who knew of the money, and the assistant should be warned not to speak about it with anyone. As far as her husband's access to it, he would have to be put on an allowance. If it sounded unreasonable to him, he should remember that they were on a tight budget and that he was too much of a spendthrift to be given free rein. She would start him off at two hundred dollars a day. It seemed fair. Did he agree or disagree? Why wasn't he answering her?

"Ben, are you listening to me?"

Ben rose from the stool. At first he seemed lost, confused even. Then his forefinger on the left hand came to sit beneath his nose and the other hand fell on his hip and his eyes shut. From the back of his throat came a peculiar bearish noise. His legs were long, his spine arched. It had occurred to him that the chicken carcass he'd thrown in the garbage five minutes before had another use, and he went to retrieve it from the can beneath the sink.

"What are you doing?" his wife asked him.

Ben told her to mind her business.

She said, "I was talking to you."

"Well, it can wait."

"Wait for what?"

Ben didn't answer. He filled a pot with water and placed it on the stovetop. Once the water was boiling, he dropped the chicken carcass, as well as the bones that had been on his plate, into the pot. For just over eight minutes, he stared into the pot, thinking. Then he drained the water, cleaned the remaining meat off the bones, and brought them into the studio. He found a shallow wood box one foot wide by one foot long, took some short nails and a hammer from a drawer, put everything on his desk, and began arranging the bones inside the box. The legs went along the edges, the breastbone was placed centrally, the wings stuck out from beneath the breastbone. He hammered the nails through the bones into the wood. After which he went into a back closet and found a bag of sand, and poured it over the bones until they were halfway submerged. Then he had Jerome cut a piece of glass, which the artist glued to the box, closing in the bones and sand.

He handed his assistant the finished piece and said, "We'll take it to the warehouse next week."

"Okay, Ark."

Overwhelmed by a powerful need for sleep, Ben went to sit in his office at the back of the loft, and within seconds he was leaning back in his chair with his eyes closed and head dropped between his shoulders, arms hanging at his sides. Every so often the sound of his breath was interrupted by a violent cough, followed by a pitiful whimper, and then a sonorous in- and exhalation. After ten minutes, Ben woke. But what had his wife been saying just moments before? He would be put on an allowance? Ben scratched behind his ear and a scab came off, which he rolled between his fingertips. Two hundred a day, was it? This sum wasn't nearly enough. His art supplies alone were seven to eight thousand a month. His junk buying and dollar-store expenditures were another two thousand. Was she including Jerome in this total? For years Eliza had been trying to get Ben to let go of his assistant. The artist wouldn't discuss it. Besides, whether or not she understood, Jerome did so much more for the Arkins than just help Ben with his art. He was their chauffeur, plumber, house painter, their muscle, their pool guy and maid. If Ben sent Jerome away, who would take on all of those responsibilities? Not Ben. Would Eliza really want her husband doing the driving? He hadn't operated a vehicle in New York City for over five years. He would kill them. Moreover, their home would fall into disrepair. And they'd break their backs carrying their bags from the trunk of the car into the loft. No, they couldn't fire Jerome. Their need for him was too great. If anything, perhaps Violet could be sent away, and Jerome could be both his assistant and Eliza's nurse. Violet was the most costly of their expenses. Why, she worked twenty-four hours a day, every day, and was paid twelve dollars an hour. That added up to more than a hundred thousand a year. As Ben conceived of it, Jerome could be with him during the mornings, pausing on occasion to look in on Eliza, and then spend the afternoons through the evenings attending to his wife. This would equal huge savings.

Ben went to discuss the matter with his wife. In the darkened living room, between wall-to-wall art, he could hear Eliza and Violet talking in the kitchen. His wife was complaining about his shopping. Wasn't she? He listened closely. Yes, she said it was obscene. And had Violet ever met a person who spent so much money on nothing? And was he not trying to put them in the poorhouse? True or false?

"And don't say false, Violet."

Without hearing her answer, Ben ran his tongue across his front teeth, deciding that the nurse would be dismissed. Not only was she too expensive, she was putting bad ideas in his wife's head. He would tell Eliza about it tonight. If she was so intent on saving money, then she wouldn't argue against it.

The artist brought his hands through his hair, clearing his throat. There was the sound of the ringing telephone. Jerome answered the phone, and was now shouting from the other room:

"Hey, Ark! It's your daughter."

"What?" Ben screamed.

"Sondra's on the phone," the assistant replied.

"Sondra?"

"Yes. Sondra!"

"Well, hang up!"

"She says she has to talk to you!"

"So what?"

"She says it's important!"

"And?"

"And just pick up the phone, Ark."

"Jesus!" Ben snatched the portable off the stand. Meandering toward the studio at the front of the loft, Ben began yelling at his eldest daughter, "I'm working, Sondra! What do you want?"

"Daddy. I'm sorry to interrupt you. I'm very, very sorry," she was saying.

"What is it?"

"You have to help me."

"What? What? Out with it!"

"Daddy, it's Doris."

"Mm."

"Daddy, she's ruining the business I built. I spent thirty-five years killing myself at *Shout!*, running that record label, and here she comes along and starts up her *Doris Arkin Shouts!*, stealing away my business, and there's no way I can stand by and let that happen."

Rain pelted the studio windows. Ben pressed the left side of his face against the cool, wet glass. But what was this about? Did Sondra mean what she was saying? Ben wasn't convinced that Sondra had done anything for the record label. Hard work was beneath her. Besides, *he* had built the company, bankrolling the first twenty of its thirty-five-year run. Giving eighty thousand in 1972 to start the business, a total that had included a salary for his son and two daughters. In 1973, *Shout!* had cost Ben another eighty thousand. In '74, sixty thousand. In '75, after finding some critical success with one of its artists and looking to increase their publicity and marketing operations, a hundred and fifty thousand. And then, for years after, while the children would swear to their father that they had at long last found the one who had not only written a record for the ages but had big earning potential, Ben had continued to hand over more money. He'd put at least two million into *Shout!* Although back in the '70s and early '80s, before *Shout!* had become profitable, Ben had found it well worth the price. Just to keep the kids busy. Employed. On a path. To give shape to their lives. For that he'd been willing to pay dearly. Who knew where they would have been or what they would have been doing otherwise, perhaps jobless, and coming by his home every day to chat. No, the alternative would have been much more costly to him.

Ben said to his daughter, "Let's talk facts. Your sister, Doris, is at work on her new label. She's a tiger, and you should be proud to call her a relation. Your brother, Oliver, is living with his new wife in Los Angeles doing God knows what. And *you*, what are you doing? Bitterly tending to your garden in Scarsdale, bored to tears and looking for a fight, I take it?"

From the kitchen, Eliza had gotten on the phone. She said, "Sondra, you're over sixty-two now. You have to start behaving like an adult."

"Mommy, you would never say that to Doris, and she acts like a little child."

"You should go on vacation, travel the world," Eliza said. She was making an effort to go easy on her daughter. The artist's wife couldn't tolerate complaint. She imagined her own great strength was for knowing a real problem when she saw one, and she expected as much from her children. She decided Oliver and Doris had some talent for it, but that Sondra had always possessed a deficiency. Honestly, how many times did a mother have to say "stop exaggerating" or "just ignore it" before it got through her kid's head? Eliza wondered how much a parent could really do for a child, anyway. It was not her life. Sondra had to learn for herself how to be. Taking a stool beneath her and relieving her legs from the effort put forth in standing, she said, "Darling, you should know you're embarrassing yourself."

"Mother."

"And we support Doris in her new label."

"Well, you've never opposed her."

"Why should we? *Shout!* has been fading for years. Doris came to us and said that she'd like to move on and did we believe in her and would we lend her money to start a new business."

"Lend her money?"

"Yes."

"What does that mean!"

"It means we gave her the money to start her company. Two hundred thousand dollars."

"You gave her two hundred thousand dollars? Are you joking? That isn't right, Mommy."

"Why not?"

"Because it isn't!"

"Bring it up with your head-doctor, Sondra."

"Oh, Mother, please!"

Pacing beneath a weeping willow in her front yard, Sondra was telling herself that as life pertained to her mother and father she was ready to complete the journey of disconnection she'd set out on long ago as a child. The memory of her father pulling over on the Long Island Expressway and ordering his three misbehaving children from the car came to mind. Before speeding off and leaving them to suffer beneath a July sun, Ben had said, "It was nice knowing you kids. Now scram!" At the next exit he'd circled back around. But the time it had taken for that to happen had been, unlike for her brother and sister, some of the happiest minutes of Sondra's life. She'd looked at Oliver and Doris, the two of them crying out for their mother and father, and thought, *We're free now. I'll raise you and do it the right way. The three of us can have a great life together. We don't need them.* Though she'd been a mere twelve years old, and the idea of bringing up her siblings had been farfetched, in returning to the memory, as often happened, a part of her always re-experienced the disappointment of her father and mother swinging back to get them.

"Well," Sondra was saying, "you have to help me stop Doris. You own thirty percent of *Shout!* and I need you to back me. If you say no, well, then…then I'm going to have to view it as an aggressive strike against me. And I'll have to sue you."

"You'll sue me?" Ben said.

"What are you talking about, Sondra?" her mother demanded.

"I'm sorry. I have to protect myself. Business was once your life, Daddy, and you were very successful. This is business. You understand. I know you do. I mean, what would you do if you were me? I have a right to save my company."

Ben, offering the last words he'd ever speak to his daughter, told her, in a whisper, "Don't call this number again."

"Sondra, you should think very hard and long about whatever this nonsense is," Eliza said.

"I have!"

"Well, maybe you want to keep thinking."

And then Ben screamed, "Eliza, hang up the fucking phone. Now!"

II. THANKS FOR LUNCH

Oliver Arkin was calling his daughter, Rebecca. The sky was so clear that Catalina was visible in the distance. But Oliver's eyes were closed. With his free hand, he reached up to the branches of an avocado tree to pluck the first ingredient for his home-made guacamole. His wife, Sheila, raved about his guacamole. And after her heart attack, he'd made it his job to stay on top of her diet. Good cholesterol, bad cholesterol—Oliver had made extensive lists. Now that he'd retired from the record industry, he had time for this sort of thing. Growing cilantro, too. He'd given that Mexican guy who did yardwork across the road seven bucks, and the lifelong New Yorker had been taught how to plant anything in soil. Turned out, Oliver had a passion for gardening. And it wasn't even that hard. After moving to Los Angeles and leaving his sisters to run the label, it had been important to him to find new interests. His wife owned two boutiques. As much as possible, Oliver resisted that work. Oliver Arkin did not sell retail. He'd started one of the most important record labels of the late '70s. *The Village Voice* had once put him on a list of the one hundred and one most influential New Yorkers. Back then, Oliver had known people and *people* had known him. Oh, discovering new talent. Had there been anything better? When it hit you in the gut? When it could not be denied? What a time he'd had, out every night, going, going, going. Why sleep? He'd had so much energy then.

And now?

Beyond guacamole, he had other new hobbies. There were wonderful seashells down on the beach. He imagined his collection was as good as any. He had discovered a mirror in a dumpster behind a Chevron station the other day, brought it home, and had been gluing seashells to the mirror's wooden frame. He would hang the finished work with twine from the avocado tree and this way, if he were seated at the picnic table and facing east, he would still be able to see the ocean in the mirror's reflection. Sure, Oliver dug the fresh air, the migrating birds, whales, and humans. Go West! Of course, he would never get a driver's license. But California suited him just fine. The thing was, at sixty years old, he had a new respect for slowing down. What had he been in such a rush about all his life anyway, never able to stop for a minute, always thinking about the next? What of now? He had been learning throughout his time in L.A. to focus on the second at hand, to quit running away from the present as if it were some contagious, life-threatening disease. He had been meditating daily. It was difficult, this cross-legged pose with the palms up on knees, the quieting of the mind and remaining still. The letting go. He had come to realize that his best friend had, in fact, been his worst enemy— namely, his neurotic mind—and that it was very hard to say goodbye to it. You had to want it, first and foremost, and not in any casual way. However, Oliver was deeply attracted to mania. It wasn't just glamorous, but delicious, too.

And so, yes, if he were being perfectly honest, he had been pleased, in part, to learn this morning that his sister, Sondra, was suing him. He had even said thank you to the man who'd shown up at his door, a kind of Dom DeLuise lookalike, to serve him with papers. No question, ninety percent of his being, give or take a percentage point, was appalled by his sister's behavior. Sondra appeared intent on destroying him. But that remaining ten percent, give or take a point, had been delighted. After the process server left, Oliver had gone into the kitchen of his large ranch-style home, squeezed six oranges, downed the fresh juice, and, savoring the last drops, begun to feel himself coming back to life. Had he been less than alive? Looking at the truth of it, not less than alive, just experiencing a deep state of boredom since beginning this new life. Christ, he was not ready to die. To fade away. He wanted action.

With his daughter Rebecca now on the line, he told her the news: Sondra was suing him, his wife, his parents, and his sister. Wasn't it outrageous? Could she imagine what it was like to be subject to this kind of aggression by a sibling? To think he had always felt guilty for having never given Rebecca a brother or sister. No more. She should consider herself one of the lucky ones. Why, who knew what kind of trials she might have had to endure had he and her mother reproduced a second or third time? There was no predicting it. Rebecca didn't have to thank him. But she should reconsider all her mentions of childhood loneliness and boredom and how she would have so enjoyed the presence of a sibling. Because the burdens of having two sisters had long outweighed the benefits. Rebecca didn't know. She couldn't understand. But it was a fact.

"Sondra is trying to put me and my parents in the grave!"

Rebecca was in the middle of lunch. The man keeping her company was Randy Nobel, her colleague at the firm. Nobel looked like Teddy Roosevelt without the glasses. The mustache was the same. Like the explorer-president, he was short, and his wardrobe was all Rough Rider, with the red cravat tied around the neck, the brown slouch hat, the shirt blue and flannel with bright gold buttons, along with the trousers and boots. He had broad shoulders and light eyes and full blond sideburns. They were at Carnegie Deli, and Nobel had put a generous feast on the table: a Nosh, Nosh Nanette, a Millie's Stuffed Cabbage. He seemed to mind being made to wait. What could she do about that? For ten minutes her father had been calling her. She'd had to answer. Clearly, it had been an emergency. But was Nobel sincerely angry? With a hundred more interesting places to rest his gaze, he was staring at her with a strange intensity. He might consider looking at the child at the adjacent table trying to stretch his mouth around his pastrami sandwich. Surely, this was more compelling than the vision of Rebecca on the phone.

Oliver was now asking his daughter how his sister could sue him for improper use of the *Shout!* corporate credit card.

"Improper *what*, Dad?" The restaurant was loud, and it was hard to hear.

"Improper use of the corporate credit card," Oliver said. "And it's truly amazing how she, who expensed Range Rovers and ski trips for her family in the Alps, could come at me for this. It's bullshit. Utter bullshit. She says she saw me misuse our credit cards all the time. Of course, what else would she be doing if not dreaming up bullshit? Certainly she had nothing to do at the company. With no personality, no worthwhile ideas, she was of no use to us. Though she tells me, 'Please, *Shout!* wouldn't have survived half as long if not for the deals I made.' 'The deals you made?' I say. '*You?* You made no deals. But don't lie, you did expense cars and trips, gifts and groceries, flowers, health spas, stays for your dog at the kennel, nose jobs, mustache bleachings, everything. Doris and I never looked at the bills. That, conveniently enough, was your job, which you did so well—bravo. And to sue your own father and mother! Do you want to bring a curse on your house? Really, Sondra. Don't do this.'"

"Dad," Rebecca interrupted, "I don't know what you're talking about. You have to slow down." Then, to Nobel, she said, "I'm sorry."

"It's not a problem," he answered. Then he set his fork and knife on the table, adjusted the brim of his hat, and shifted back in his chair into a casual half-sitting, half-reclining posture.

Oliver was talking again of how he'd never given Rebecca siblings. He said he finally understood why. Yes, he'd foreseen just this sort of thing happening to her. That, despite his excellent parenting and his daughter being of sound mind, Rebecca would have likely woken one morning some twenty years from now to find that her brother or sister was declaring a perverse sort of war against her. Indeed, he knew just how it would have gone.

"You're an Arkin. This is what we get."

There had been a long history of battles between family members. Any details which Oliver had stored in his mind now came out, helter skelter. He mentioned names of uncles and aunts and cousins and cousins once removed that were unfamiliar to Rebecca. Had Rebecca noticed how few extended family members were in attendance at any of the weddings and funerals? Had she thought about why?

"Lawsuits are your answer!"

Rebecca told Nobel, "Go ahead and eat. It's okay. I have to leave," and she took her purse and coat and went out on Seventh Avenue. The city air seemed to hum at a decibel that canceled out her father's voice. She covered her ear and turned the corner, finding a doorway to stand in.

Oliver was saying, "Your grandparents gave Doris two hundred thousand dollars to start a new company. But should they have had to ask Sondra if it was okay with her?"

"Dad, start over. I missed everything you just said."

"It's ridiculous. Completely and totally ridiculous. And I told Sondra...I told her, 'You've got to be out of your fucking mind. You'll sue Mom and Dad for illegally competing against their own business. That's what you'll make of their giving Doris money? I mean, please. Can you try and be a little fucking honest with yourself? You're doing this because you're angry about where we are and what we're doing, that each of us are thriving while you're just getting fat in suburbia.' Sixteen million she wants from your grandparents. *Sixteen million*! And four million from me."

"Four million!"

"Yes."

Rebecca had to be back at her office in thirty minutes. Seeing a taxi, she got in the car and told the driver, "Fiftieth and Lexington."

"And I said to her...I said, 'Do you want us on the streets? Haven't you been to enough therapists to be beyond this bitterness? What about the medication, the yoga retreats, the water aerobics, is none of it helping?' She's even suing my wife. After being single for more than twenty years, I finally *get* married and she wants to do my marriage in. You know, I wish your grandfather hadn't missed her birth."

"Missed her birth, Dad?"

"Have you never heard the story? When your grandmother was having Sondra, Ben was at a double feature around the corner from the hospital."

"And?"

"*And* it says everything to Sondra about how little her father's cared for her and how she's been deprived of his love. She's always preferred to make excuses for herself rather than face the truth."

"Dad—"

"But what a critic she's been of your grandparents since the beginning. I remember...I remember this doll she had. This Baby Clara. With that piece of plastic your aunt would instruct your grandmother about the correct way to hold, to feed, to clothe, to burp, to change, and to comfort a child. No wait... wait, and there'd been this day that Doris had torn off Baby Clara's arms, and...and Sondra had hurried in a taxi to the New York Doll Hospital on Lexington."

This had been a business in the lower sixties, a second-floor operation overlooking the bus-and-cab jammed avenue which had specialized in fixing dolls. Irving Chais, the head surgeon, had told Sondra, already fifteen years old, to go up the street to Bloomingdale's and shop while he operated. At the department store, Sondra had bought herself a pair of Holly Golightly Oliver Goldsmith sunglasses while Chais repaired the doll.

"...And what a speech she delivered to your grandmother when she got home: This was how you dealt with children in an emergency. This was the kind of attention she would provide her own sons and daughters. This was parenting."

"Dad, I—"

"She always has been a righteous bitch."

"Dad!"

"And nothing will hold up in court. She doesn't have a case. That's what my wife says, anyway."

"Well, your wife is not a lawyer. I'm the lawyer. I'm going to help you with this, Dad."

Oliver went through the large sliding-glass door into the kitchen to brew himself his fifth and sixth espresso shots of the morning. The machine grinded the beans and brewed the drink with the push of a button. He shook two Sweet'n'Low packets in the air, saying to his daughter, "On top of that, Rebecca, the stores are a total bust. Every month they lose more and more money. No one's spending now. I don't know what we'll do. I almost asked to borrow money from you last month. But Sheila—she has such pride, she wouldn't let me."

Rebecca knew nothing of her father's finances. She had always assumed his wife, Sheila, was comfortable. After all, they lived on a beautiful piece of property on the Pacific, in Malibu. She said, "Dad, I do well. Not *that* well. I have a mortgage, you know. I couldn't keep you guys in business. You might consider closing the stores."

"Obviously! But Sheila doesn't know when to admit defeat. She's spending everything on these boutiques. She says things will turn around."

"And if they don't?"

"I don't know. I mean, we'll manage. We'll do something! Right now my concern is with your grandfather. He's having a very hard time with this. You should go see him."

Rebecca straightened her legs across the back seat of the taxi. She said, "I'd like to, Dad. I'm so busy at work. I hardly have a minute to myself. I sleep some nights at the office, in my chair."

"But you'll try and make the time?"

"I mean...yes, I will. I'm sure this whole suit is a total nightmare for him."

"You don't even know the half of it."

Back at the office, Rebecca took a toothbrush, floss, and toothpaste from her desk and went to the bathroom. Staring into the mirror above the sink, she brought the floss between her crooked front teeth, taking note of her face. The severely tired dark eyes were a frightful sight of rapid aging and distress. The long black hair had been neglected for months. Her skin was flaky, her neck streaked with red marks from nervous scratching. She washed her face. Beneath long fingers, the roughness of her cheeks provided yet another reason to wince.

After work, she changed into running clothes and jogged three miles through Central Park. She stretched afterward, in a yoga class. Back at her apartment, she took a bath. The hot water and green-tiled walls and the closed bathroom door quieted the part of her mind that could not stop going even in exhaustion. She put a wet cloth over her eyes. There was a glass of red wine on the sink, and, stepping out of the bath a moment later, she drank the wine down fast.

Tonight I'll sleep, she told herself.

In bed, however, she was restless. The sheets pricked at her. The pillow lumped at her neck. Rebecca hung a sock over the red light of the alarm clock, but she could still feel the growing lateness of the hour. How much longer would she lie frustrated like this? When would she give up on sleep? At some point, it was only logical to get out of bed, turn on the lights, and submit to insomnia.

And so she did.

The blue jeans and black sweater at the top of the hamper were clean enough, and she pulled herself into the clothes and went down the hall with a bottle of red wine to see her neighbor, Gertrude Fish. It was almost 1:30 a.m., but Gertrude kept odd hours. You couldn't expect her to be up before noon, yet in the middle of night she was exuberant, chirping, and a little mad. Through the door, Rebecca could hear the old woman sanding wood. Rebecca rang the bell twice. It was after the third attempt that Gertrude chortled, then screamed, "Who is it!"

"It's Rebecca."

"Rebecca? Oh. Hi. Yes."

The door opened, and Gertrude removed her white medical mask and purple latex gloves and ordered her neighbor inside.

From the foyer, Rebecca saw furniture in the process of being constructed and finished pieces yet to be picked up by Gertrude's clients, as well as books and more books stacked in tall piles on the floor. The classical radio station was playing an Ives symphony. Gertrude made Rebecca sit in a chair covered in sawdust. There was a sinister quality to Gertrude's face. Short, tangled gray hair capped her five-foot frame. Her midsection had the slope and broadness of an old cash register. She wore a black turtleneck, brown corduroy pants, orthopedic shoes. It was her work outfit. She was working. Gertrude maintained a woodshop in her apartment, her style simple and attractive, functional. The noise generated from her electric saws and sanders, coupled with the toxic stains and finishes whose odors wafted into the hallway, didn't help Gertrude's status in the building. The co-op board had tried to put a stop to her operation many times. They threatened eviction. She bribed board presidents, not with cash—she didn't have much of that—but with the refurbishing of a rocking chair, the construction of a child's bed, a side table, an outdoor bench. They were astonished by Gertrude's skill at carpentry. Met throughout her life with low expectations—by her mother and father, in particular—Gertrude was used to this kind of treatment.

When Rebecca moved into her apartment three years before, a neighbor had warned her to stay away from Gertrude Fish. She had said that Gertrude "isn't all there." Compared with "batty," "deranged," "a scare," "bad for real estate value," and "disruptive," it was one of the nicer ways Rebecca had heard Gertrude described. As it was, the carpenter disliked her fellow tenants more. How many times had she explained to Rebecca that in 1974, when she'd first moved in, people like herself had occupied half the apartments, but that time had long since passed. That now you had to be a millionaire and have a second house even to get an interview. That they wouldn't let people of color or queers buy. That they were afraid of them, and that they were also afraid of her. And that Gertrude thought that they should be, because she despised them. It seemed she brought it up during every visit.

Gertrude handed Rebecca a wine screw. "Do the honors, please."

Rebecca uncorked the bottle. There were two glasses on a small table beside her. She poured the wine, and they touched glasses.

"You know, before you showed up, Rebecca, I was working on a chair, and I became so distracted by the word 'fornicate' I almost took off another finger." She held up her left hand. Half the middle finger was missing. She had accidentally sliced it off with a saw years before. "It's one of my favorite words in the whole English language. Don't you just love it? Say it, Rebecca. *Fornicate.*"

Rebecca indulged her neighbor. "Fornicate."

"It makes the whole mouth come alive, doesn't it? God, I love that word. You know, you're very pretty. You're very pretty!" She was like a cuckoo clock when she said it, her eyes and mouth convulsing, and her voice reaching up two octaves. Suddenly, Gertrude got up from her seat and went back into her shop. When she returned, she handed Rebecca a footstool made of a dark wood. This wasn't a breezily nailed together object. Hard work was evident in the details.

"It's beautiful, Gertrude."

"You said you had nothing to elevate your feet at work."

Mother of pearl was embedded over the screwheads. Rebecca's initials were monogrammed on top. She said, "You made this for me?"

"I hope it serves you well. Now, give me more wine!"

Rebecca raised the bottle and poured. Gertrude took the cork and pushed it back in the bottle. She said, "I can't stand it when people don't put the cork back in. Maybe that makes me anal. But what reason do I have to be that? Am I holding shit up there?" She rose from her seat and tapped her posterior. "Must be, you know?"

All of a sudden, Rebecca said, "I got a strange call from my father today. His sister, she's suing him. She's suing the whole family, actually. My dad was telling me all about it. He seemed out of his mind."

Gertrude's eyelids fluttered. She said, "Describe your father."

"My dad? Oh, well, he's sensitive and prone to instability. He's not weak exactly, not a coward. But when faced with adversity, he tends to run the other way. He lost his mind once before."

"Did he ever find it?"

"Most of it."

"But not all?"

Rebecca shook her head.

"You expect he'll band together with his parents?"

"Maybe," Rebecca said. "But probably not. With these people, it's all irrationality and destruction. It was so hard for him to break free of his family. It took him fifty-eight years to do it. Working with his sisters all his life, and with his parents part owners in the company controlling everyone and everything, and my father being so susceptible to their influence. They rode him hard. His sisters, too. Being in business with these people meant getting hammered down on every day for thirty-five years straight. The screaming, the violence. I remember my dad coming home with a black eye one day. Sondra—she sucker punched him. She had a diamond ring on her finger, too, and he had to get six stitches. But he went back to work

the next day and fell right into line. He would never leave.
Until two and a half years ago, that is, when he remarried. At
the time he was this big," Rebecca said, holding her fingers
close together. "But after moving to Los Angeles—his wife is
from there—and cutting off the yoke, he became something of
a whole person again."

"You don't visit him, do you?"

"Occasionally. My mother's in L.A., too."

"But you would never live there. Well, why would you? Your
whole family's left. You've got the whole city to yourself. So,
what's wrong with this aunt of yours?"

"My aunt?" Rebecca took a drink of wine, thinking. "Between all her parents' children, she's the un-pretty one. She's
not as likeable as her siblings, either. She's a bully, like her dad."

"Mmm."

"And she has no relationship with her parents. She doesn't
see them more than once a year. I don't think they talk on the
phone very much. And then, her parents have a lot of money.
She might think she's been cut out of the will—for all I know,
she has been—and she could be trying to get hers. Gertrude, I
want to help my dad."

"I never had that problem."

"Well, I've been very selfish over the last fifteen years, and
that's had its uses. But I've never done anything important for
my father. Maybe I can help him win this lawsuit. I can put
him in touch with the right people. I can direct him. My grandparents, too."

"Did they ask for your help?"

"No. But in their minds, I'm still a child. It would never
occur to them."

"Maybe they don't want your counsel. I say, sit back. Wait
for them to ask. Don't insert yourself into their problems."

"So, you think I should just keep on living my life as if none of this were happening?"

"For as long as you can," Gertrude said. "Yes. That's exactly what you should do."

III. APRÈS LE DÉLUGE

Summer moved along, and Ben did his best to ignore Sondra's lawsuit. He made his art. He shopped for groceries. He cooked chicken and wandered Chinatown. He thought about refrigeration. He sat at the dining table at the house in Southampton and cut obituaries for his files, dozens and dozens of them, walked on the beach at sunrise on Saturday and Sunday mornings and did his exercises there in the sand, napped in the late morning and again in the afternoon on the deck beside the pool, and sought new ways to open up his mind and give fresh energy to his body. For instance, he bought thousands of books at the Salvation Army in Hoboken—every kind of book, books of poetry and cookbooks and collections of plays and books on childcare and on mental health and encyclopedias and almanacs and dictionaries—and stacked them all over the loft, in his studio and his office and in the living room, having decided it would make him feel stronger to be surrounded by so many books. And at times, he imagined, it was working. However, neither the books, nor the exercise, nor the fresh ocean air was potent enough to combat the devastating physical and mental effects of Sondra and her lawyers, who were finding new reasons to file charges against her father and mother every other week. No, the case wasn't going away as quickly as the lawyers had originally assured him it would. In fact, Ben wasn't hearing any details about the lawsuit moving toward a conclusion. Only about new bills. It seemed he'd racked up a hundred-thousand-dollar fee in just a month. Had it been longer? Perhaps a couple of days, a week. But now, by the time July rolled around, the bill was up to one hundred and fifty thousand, and then, come August, two hundred and fifty thousand, and then four hundred thousand by September, and now six hundred thousand with the start of autumn. Ben screamed at his lawyers—what was going on! When would this stop? They told Ben that for all intents and purposes things were going briskly. His daughter was relentless. She was doing everything to protract the suit, to drain him of his financial resources and his energy. And what could they do about that?

On the late November morning that the legal bill hit eight hundred and forty thousand dollars, Ben received a call from the superintendent at his warehouse in Jersey City. The artist and his assistant were parked in the Cadillac, waiting for Eliza to finish up at the hairdresser on Mott Street. The superintendent began explaining how a week of rain had flooded the room where Ben's art was stored. He couldn't be specific about the damage to any work. He hadn't been inside to look. What he knew for sure was that there was water. And perhaps lots of it.

Jerome rushed from the car into the hairdresser's. Seeing the artist's wife seated in a black salon chair, a white barber's apron cinched at the neck, her short red hair marked with thin pieces of tinfoil, and with Violet standing at her side, Jerome, visibly breathless and shaking, explained what had happened.

"Oh," Eliza replied. There was a Band-Aid above her eyebrow. She had fallen off the bed yesterday and hit her head on the floor. Still, she looked pleased. She said, "I hope it's all washed away. It's garbage which has to be gotten rid of by someone at some point anyway."

Her position on Ben's art had long ceased to offend Jerome. But he said, "Another crisis might kill him."

"I don't see any change in my husband of late." Looking up into the mirror, Eliza said, "Do you, Violet?"

Amenable, subdued, Violet said, "No, Ms. Arkin."

"Perhaps you're not aware of how much Ben spends on that warehouse. It's three thousand and five hundred dollars a month. Running around scraping together money to pay these lawyers, and here he is wasting so much. Now he can finally get rid of the place."

"Eliza, this might kill him."

"Well, then I'll finally get to winter in Miami. You'll come with me, Violet, won't you?"

To be heard above a hair dryer, Violet leaned into the old woman's ear. She said, "Ms. Arkin, I go where you go."

"We can go anywhere. We'll have to go somewhere. I must get out of that loft. I can't live there another day. It's simply a terrible place. The moths have taken over. There's no light. I think Southampton in the summer, and Miami in the winter. What do you say, Violet?"

"Ms. Arkin, I say yes."

"My husband is not well. He should be put away and given extensive psychiatric treatment."

Jerome said, "Please, Eliza, just listen to me for a second."

"He's a danger to society, don't you think, Violet?"

"He *is* different," the nurse replied.

"You're just being nice now," Eliza said.

Jerome's dark eyes flashed a severe look. He didn't have time for this conversation. He told Eliza and Violet to take a taxi home. "I don't know when we'll be back. Maybe by six or seven o'clock."

"Take all the time in the world," Eliza told him. "We won't be waiting for you."

Fifteen minutes later, the artist and his assistant were driving through the Holland Tunnel. Neither person spoke. When Jerome couldn't endure the silence another moment, he gave Ben's knee a pat, and told him not to worry. He said, "I think you could save a lot of money putting more miles between the warehouse and the city. We should consider a move."

"Shut up," Ben said. "Don't talk."

"Go five more miles into Jersey, and the rents are half as much as what you're paying for your place."

"I said shut up!"

"But Ben, you haven't given me my salary for two weeks!"

The artist, in tunnel-flickering light, raised his left hand in the air. He had never hit Jerome. Yet he looked as if he'd strike him now. "Just drive the fucking car, you hear me!"

Jerome didn't answer.

"Do you understand!" the artist screamed.

"Yes, Ben. Yes, I do."

The artist lowered his left hand into his lap and held it tightly with the right for the duration of the drive.

The warehouse was ten minutes beyond the tunnel, on a street in Jersey City that no one would ever find unless he was looking for it. No homes nearby. No people out walking. No businesses. No life. It was a six-story white brick building surrounded by mud filled with all the toxins that gave Jersey its reputation. Jerome pulled up out front. Reynolds, the superintendent, was waiting for them on the steps, clad in a navy jumper, and with his legs pretzeled beneath a tremendous belly. Ben was always warning Jerome that if he kept eating the way he did, he'd look like the superintendent one day. And that if he didn't start using his head, he'd end up with a job like the superintendent had. However, Reynolds had always seemed happy to Jerome, significantly happier than Ben Arkin, who now came slowly from the car with his chin up high and his shoulders pulled back. He brushed past the superintendent without saying a word.

"You'll need a flashlight," the superintendent told Jerome. "I killed the power. Had to. Else there could be a fire."

"You think it's bad down there?" Jerome asked.

"Can't say," Reynolds answered. "There's water. That's all I know for sure."

Jerome could see Ben descending the stairs to the basement, and he ran to catch up but didn't get there in time. Ben opened the basement door. A surge of water rushed in past his ankles.

"Fucking shit!" Ben yelled.

"Ben, wait for me," Jerome called down from the top of the stairwell.

"Fucking mother hell."

"Just hold on a second," Jerome said.

Inside the warehouse, water came up to their thighs. The ceiling felt close. There were a few thousand works stored here. Forty years of sixteen-hour days, minus the time for the prostate cancer, the dental work, the obsessive grocery shopping, and however much more for the vacations Ms. Arkin had forced on Ben. All that life's worth of work. At least three-quarters of it was under water. That was Jerome's initial estimate when he shined a beam of light through the room. The assistant, silent, weak with fear, followed after Ben through the water. The old man struggled with each step, but was slowly getting farther and farther from the entryway. Then he waved Jerome off. He said, "Get away from me. Go. Please." Ben turned and disappeared into a corner.

Jerome shut off the flashlight then and was in darkness. It was better to wait without seeing, besides. He touched his fingertips to the water, skimming the surface, making a light splash of sound. Then he said Ben's name.

"Ben, what's going on out there? Do you need me?"

Only silence. Was he having heart attack? A stroke? No, Jerome told himself. No, not even this could kill Ben. He was the toughest man Jerome had ever known. He had starved through the Depression. His father had died before it was over. Jerome didn't know how. Ben wouldn't tell him. He didn't like to talk about his past. The assistant still imagined he knew more about Ben than most people. The artist had had two brothers, three sisters, and his mother to support by the age of fifteen. He'd graduated high school at sixteen, and had been given a position at Macy's on Thirty-Fourth Street not long after as a gofer in their ad department. Ben hadn't said much about the job. Only the cafeteria. The greatest day of his life had been when he'd first walked into the Macy's cafeteria as an employee and could eat as much of anything as he'd wanted. Every day, turkey and mashed potatoes, meatloaf, ziti, fried chicken, apple and cherry and key lime pie. He still spoke about that Macy's cafeteria. The Depression had made Arkin mad about food. Jerome drove the artist to the Shop Rite in Jersey City, where things were cheaper than in Manhattan, and he would stock up: pasta and rice, cereal, dried fruits, chocolate syrup, tomato juice, walnuts, peanuts, cashews, pecans. He didn't eat any of the food, but put it away in the warehouse in case a day should come in the future of humankind, an event so catastrophic that the whole food supply vanished. He said that being prepared for life's inevitable disasters was part of his genius. Ben had headed up his own advertising firm on Madison Avenue, sold it, and retired a multi-millionaire at forty-two. After which, he'd put himself away in the studio to become an uncivilized animal and make art with blood. Those were his words. Ben hadn't put any effort into becoming famous. Said Ben on the subject: "It's a waste of time for a genius like me to peddle his art. I say get down to the bloody work, make something the world's never seen, and when you're dead perhaps they'll find out about you—if they're lucky!"

Oftentimes, Ben would stop with his work and draw his hand through the air and say, "You see this? These paintings? These sculptures? They are perfectly meaningless things. And yet, in making them, I have felt what it feels like to be a king. And that stimulus to my brain, that knowledge of creation which I have gained…that, Jerome, is what all this making is about."

Although Jerome hadn't known the first thing about art, Ben had hired him one morning eight years ago right off Canal Street, where he'd been stripping furniture for an antique dealer. Ben had called to him from behind the wheel of his Cadillac.

He'd said, "Hey, kid, you good with your hands?"

Jerome had said he was.

"Will you work for five an hour?"

"Five twenty-five," Jerome had said.

And Ben had gone, "All right. Come on, you."

These days, Jerome was making only six-fifty, still well under the minimum wage. But then, the young man had always considered this the most interesting work a poor Puerto Rican kid from the Bronx with no education could have. Anyway, that's what Ben said, and Jerome couldn't help but agree.

Driving back from Jersey that day, Ben told Jerome he wanted him to round up some of his friends, four or five, as many as he could find. He wasn't shouting, he was very calm, in shock, Jerome thought. Ben said he should rent the biggest vacuums he could find, go into the warehouse, suck out that water, and see what they could save.

"You can tell your friends I'll give them the same I give you."

"Okay."

Jerome dropped Ben off at the curb in front of the loft. He said, "So should I bring the car back to the lot?"

Ben leaned through the passenger-side window. His round face and wide nose, the jutting lips, the dimple in his chin, the mean blue eyes, the monstrous expression of power—Jerome felt he had to show a lot of courage now just to look straight at him. The artist said, "You idiot, what the fuck did I just say? I said you'll go round up as many friends as you can. You'll rent vacuums. You'll go back to Jersey. You'll…"

"I got it. So, you want me to do that now?"

"Yes, now. What's wrong with you?"

Jerome apologized, and told Ben he could get two friends right away, that they were up in the Bronx, Grand Concourse, which was where he lived, and where, eighty-three years ago, Ben Arkin had been born. He'd have to drive up and get them, then rent vacuums. Did Ben want him to stay all night at the warehouse? Because he'd do it, for him.

And Ben said, "Yes. Do that. Now."

Jerome rode in the Cadillac to Grand Course. He saw Pedro on a corner and convinced him to help. Next, Jerome called Martin, who suggested Earl. Vic was with Earl, and both needed the money. They rented vacuums from Jose, the vacuum guy, up the street. Ben called when they were in tunnel traffic on their way back to Jersey. The assistant had heard Ben's voice after he'd found out that his eldest daughter was going to sue him, and when Ms. Arkin had nearly died of pneumonia a couple years ago, and then during 9/11 with the towers burning just south of their home. But he sounded worst of all right now. He asked Jerome, "Are you at the warehouse yet?"

Jerome said, "No."

"Why not?"

"It takes time to find manpower and vacuums. We'll be there soon."

Ben said, "I called the super and told him to turn the power back on. You'll keep the wires up out of the water, or you'll fry. How many flashlights do you have?"

"None."

Ben sighed. "How the hell are you going to work in the dark?"

"You said the power will be back on. I'll turn on the overheads."

Ben said, "All right. Fine," and he hung up.

Jerome and the crew spent the night vacuuming up the water. It seemed as if they were getting nowhere. Ben called for updates. Jerome tried to be optimistic. He told him the water was coming up—which it was, though very slowly. There was just so much of it. Like draining a pond, he told the artist. They took smoke breaks every hour on the hour. Guys went out to get coffee. At moments, they thought that maybe they were having fun. When the crew began to tire, Jerome reminded them that they were saving the artwork of the great genius, Ben Arkin, and that that was a very big deal.

"Is that true?" they asked.

"Yes," Jerome told them. "Come over here and look at this."

Jerome led the group around a hill of soggy cardboard boxes to some metal shelves. Up on top was a painting of Doris and Eliza and Eliza's brother, Gregory. Eliza was painted nude at the middle of the painting, her left hand red. Two brown horses with their heads lowered were coming in at either side of her. Gregory strummed a guitar in space just behind his sister, while in the right corner Ben's youngest child, Doris, about thirteen years old, was lying on her back in the grass, reading a letter. Green and blue paint dominated the color-scape. Jerome found the arrangement of figures eerie and sexually provocative. He told his friends that it was an important painting. And, for almost fifteen seconds, everyone stood in silence. Then Martin asked about whether or not Ben would pay them time-and-a-half.

"If I'm working here all night, I want time-and-a-half."

"Okay."

"It's against the law not to pay time-and-a-half," Martin said. Jerome promised to ask.

By four in the morning, at least half the water was gone. But what a mess. Ben didn't work small. Most of the Abstract paintings from the '80s and early '90s were done on large fifteen and twenty-foot canvases. They were waterlogged, destroyed. Jerome was distraught over *Deathbed*, a series of sculptures he and Ben had made just six months before using rusted chicken wire, sand, dirt, goat bones, and bed frames. Although the seven bed frames wrapped in chicken wire were intact, the sand, dirt, and goat bones had all been washed away. Ben had had a photography phase in the late '70s. Thousands of those photos were under water, the colors running. It was all garbage now and had to be taken to the dumpster out back behind the building.

Around noon, they returned to Wooster. Jerome went upstairs to speak with Ben, and he mentioned time-and-a-half. The artist shook his head.

"They worked all night for you, Ark. Almost twenty-four hours straight. They pulled so much out of that water. They cleaned up the warehouse."

"*Yeah!*" Ben shouted. He said, "Six-fifty an hour times twenty-three equals…" He wrote the numbers down on a yellow legal pad using a fat black marker and came up with $149.50. He reached into his pocket and took out his money clip. He peeled off five one hundred dollar bills, and said, "This is what I have right now."

"You mean you don't have the full amount!"

But Ben walked back inside his studio without answering.

Jerome paid his friends with the money, refusing his own cut, and threw the car in the lot just south of Broome, then came back to say goodbye to Ben. However, Ben told him to go back and get the car. He was irate.

"Whoever said you were supposed to put the Cadillac in the lot! We're driving out to Jersey." He wanted to assess the damage.

Jerome had been up so long, though. He told Ben, "I need to go home." He was filthy. He had to shower and sleep.

"Get the fucking car!"

Jerome told him, "Ben, I have to go home."

"So you're telling me you quit?"

"What?"

"Are you telling me you quit?"

"Ark."

"Well, are you?"

Minutes later, they were driving back through the Holland Tunnel. Ben ate sunflower seeds, spitting the shells on the floor. Jerome would have to clean them up. In the past, the assistant had tried everything to get the artist to dispose of the seeds in a container. There were paper cups in the glove compartment, a trash basket at his feet. Jerome had begged him to use these, but he couldn't get the artist to listen.

At the warehouse, Ben surveyed the wreckage, his head up and his hands behind his back. Every so often he stopped at a work and looked for a few seconds, then continued on without saying anything. There were more than a hundred pieces stored high above the floor which had been spared. Jerome mentioned these as a way of being positive.

Ben scowled. He said, "You're not an artist."

"No."

"That's why you don't know that this is all just meaningless. I've told you before and I'll tell you again...these are just meaningless objects. It's the experience of making the work. That's the thing!"

Ben was violently wiping the corners of his mouth with his thumb and forefinger. Jerome put a cigarette between his lips, lit it, shielding his eyes. He wouldn't look at the artist.

"Yes, I was there for the creation," Ben continued. "That's what it's about, Jerome. The rest...the rest is all a lot of bullshit."

IV. FILIAL PIETY

In January, Oliver Arkin flew from Los Angeles to New York. He'd sold his apartment on East Eightieth Street. He had wanted a million and a quarter for the property and had spent weeks telling his wife how he wouldn't take a penny less. Why, he'd lived there for almost thirty years. He had raised Rebecca in those rooms. She had learned to walk and talk, to count, dress, and read there. What a time they'd had over the years. Selling it for less would be an insult to that past. However, in the end, he'd accepted $910,000. He hadn't received any better offers. And he needed the money.

Oliver wandered the rooms of the apartment. Seeing everything he would have to pack up—the records and books, the pots and pans, glasses and dishware, the clothes, the furniture, the shelves in the living room, the desk, the piano—he felt sick. How would he even begin to look through all the drawers and closets? He had to be out of the place in six days. It wasn't enough time. The money from the sale of the apartment had yet to come through, and he didn't have enough in his accounts to pay for movers. Maybe he would walk his chairs and bookcases and lamps out to the street. The dining set was valuable. The chandeliers were very good. But why hold onto any of the old stuff? He had no use for it.

He sighed, pumping his hands on his waist. Now he called Rebecca. She was at the office. She said she couldn't talk for long.

"Dad, I'm sorry about this. But think of it this way: you don't live in New York anymore. Los Angeles is your home."

"I know," he replied. "You're right. You're absolutely right."

He asked Rebecca if she'd like to come over and take anything. There was so much. Did she want a couch or a bed or a medicine cabinet or a set of window curtains or a folding table? Rebecca said she had already been to the apartment weeks before and had gone through her closets and drawers. She had donated clothes to the Goodwill on Second Avenue, and thrown away plenty.

"It felt good," she told her father.

And it bolstered him to hear her say so.

Oliver started talking about Sondra then. He said his sister would rot in hell for what she had done to her parents, that God would punish her.

"What is the latest with the case?"

"The latest?"

"Yes."

But at the next moment Oliver began apologizing to his daughter. He was explaining how he'd been in the process of selling the apartment, his head had been in a million places at one time, he should have told her, he had meant to but he'd forgotten. Yes, all counts brought by Sondra against her parents and siblings and Sheila had been dismissed by the judge. The suit was over. They had won.

At her desk, her body still and heart calm, Rebecca congratulated her father. But she felt neither relief nor excitement. Pushing back in her chair, she tapped the heels of her feet and closed her eyes.

"Did Ben say anything to you about me speaking to his attorneys?"

"No."

"He called about two months ago and asked if I would talk to them and make sure they weren't overbilling. I meant to do it. It's just, I've had so much work."

"He's never brought it up, honey."

"The thing is," Rebecca continued, "there was nothing I could have done. Just because I'm a lawyer, it doesn't mean I know when another lawyer is ripping off his client."

"That makes sense."

"I wish I had done a lot more."

"We won, didn't we?"

"But the bill to the lawyer is enormous."

"That's not your problem."

"No, except—"

"Don't worry about it, please. You have a life."

"I know, but—"

"These are not your problems, Rebecca."

"Okay, Dad."

Over the next four hours, Oliver rode the elevator up and down with his things, walked them outside, and left them on the sidewalk halfway up the block. It was a fact that, in New York City, no discarded furniture ever remained on the sidewalks for more than a minute or two before it was whisked away by a new owner. And indeed, each time Oliver returned with the next items, the last of it was already gone. However, after forty minutes of transferring rugs and televisions, cushions and mirrors, a film projector and a drink trolley through the basement door out onto the sidewalk, Oliver decided he was too old for this kind of work. He asked Larry, the night guy, if he wanted a Cuisinart. How about a shoe rack? Or a microwave?

"You can have it all. Would you want to come by tomorrow and take it?"

Indeed, Larry, the night guy, arrived at 10 a.m. the following day with four friends. They were as good as professionals. The whole apartment was packed up in hours. The final boxes went out toward late afternoon. Oliver went room to room, making sure nothing had been left behind. The place—now completely empty—felt twice as large. Oliver felt big. Well, he was a big person. His six foot three inches and broad shoulders disguised a soft belly, a meaty backside. His hands and feet were considerable. His nose and ears, too. *But this openness,* he thought, *must have been what I first fell in love with when I bought the apartment.*

He sat down on the dining room floor. Leaning into his hands, he looked overhead at a black wire that coiled out of a hole in the ceiling. A silver-plated, bell-shaped chandelier had been there for two decades. It now belonged to Larry, the night guy. But he could remember when he and Rebecca's mother had bought this place. They'd had a lot of fine ideas about what to do with it. And they had done it all. "Don't marry an actress," his father had told him. And what had Oliver said in return? "I'm the better actor."

He said it now, rising to his feet. But what he needed was to leave here. He didn't feel like himself at the moment, and why prolong this mood?

He took a taxi downtown to his parents' loft. His father let him in the door. Oliver followed the artist through a dark hallway into the kitchen. He was thanking Ben for letting him stay a few nights. His father said nothing.

Ben had been in the kitchen eating chicken before his son had shown up. During their sixty-four years of marriage, Eliza had accused her husband of poisoning her with his cooking many times. Ben never read expiration dates. He didn't mind eating spoiled food. The chicken on the kitchen counter had a bad look to it. There wasn't much meat left on the bones. Ben chewed the wings, sucked marrow from the drumsticks. He turned the chicken over and ate at its underside. Oliver watched. He had seen his father devour many chickens this way. It wasn't the kind of thing you ever got used to. Finished eating, the artist washed his face at the sink and then dried himself with a towel.

Oliver began to ask about his mother. He would like to say hello to her. Was she awake? He could hear the television on at the back of the loft.

"You sold the apartment?" Ben said, all of a sudden. Ben's almost circular head was resting on his knuckles.

Oliver said that it was sold, yes. No turning back. That was it. At the next moment, he started discussing Sondra. He had written her a letter. Told her never to contact him. He hadn't heard back. But had she nothing to say? That would be a first. With a mouth like hers. Could Ben imagine it? Sondra, rendered speechless?

"How much did you get?" his father asked him.

"What's that?"

"I asked you how much you got for the apartment."

Oliver's head moved side to side. His gaze rose toward the ceiling. He appeared to be counting. In fact, his mind was a blank.

"I asked you how much."

"About nine hundred thousand before taxes."

Ben's mouth stretched wide. His tongue licked at the corners. Then he said, "Well, you'll give me that money."

"Give it to you?"

"Yes."

"Dad—"

"You heard me. I want that money."

"Hold on. Just hold on. Dad, how much do you need?"

"Every cent."

"Dad, that's not possible."

"I owe the lawyers a million."

"What about selling the loft?"

"Fuck you. And live where?"

"You could take out money against Southampton."

"I already have."

"There's a lien on Southampton?"

"Hey, it isn't yours yet!"

"Dad, please. You know I didn't mean that. Look, I sold the apartment because I don't have any money. How do you expect me to eat?"

"Your wife's rich, isn't she?"

"Not like I thought. She has property. She'll have to sell it soon to pay off her debts. After that money runs out, I don't know what we'll do. The boutiques were a colossal failure. I told her to stop, but she kept doubling down."

"That's got nothing to do with me. You sold your apartment. You'll give me that money."

"Dad!"

"*What?* Remember who paid for you to start that record label! Remember who financed the whole thing for fifteen years before you could pull your shit together and make a dime! I gave you kids millions so you could have a goddamn life. Now you'll give me that money, or you can forget about an inheritance."

Throughout the years, his father hadn't shown any bitterness toward *Shout!* Oliver had never seen Ben's financial backing as anything but belief in the company and its mission. He wouldn't think anything differently now. He said, "Dad, if I give you that money, I'll be ruined."

"You'll be all right."

"Not if I give you everything I have."

"You'll get it back soon enough."

"But what about now? Oh, Dad, come on. I need that money to live!"

"*I* need it to live!"

"Well, how about half of what I get after taxes? How about that?"

However, Ben said, "No. I want it all." Then he walked off toward the back of the loft.

Oliver followed after him, protesting. But then suddenly he was quiet. There was his mother, lying on the sofa. Seeing her son, she reached out her hands, and Oliver took them. He kissed her on the forehead.

"How are you, Mom? It's great to see you. I've missed you so much."

Eliza touched his cheek. She kept her hand there, gazing at her son. Her eyes were wet with tears at one moment, but at the next they were scanning Oliver's body. She pointed out that his shirt and his jeans were black. "Oliver, darling, the drivers won't be able to see you. They'll plow right into you. Ben, bring me one of your red flannel shirts. Oliver has to borrow it."

"What?" Ben called from the other room.

"Your red flannel shirt! Bring it to me."

"Mom, don't strain yourself. It's okay. I'm not going to get run over."

"But it's almost dusk. How will the drivers see you? They won't. Just borrow the shirt, please. Ben! Ben! Bring me the shirt, please."

"Mom, you know Dad's hard of hearing."

"Then go into his closet and take it yourself. For me, please. I'll sleep better."

Oliver put his lips to his mother's hands. "All right," he told her. "I'll do it. You don't have to worry."

"Thank you," she said, smiling at her son. She asked him about his apartment. So the place had been vacated. Was he all right? He had spent so many years there. Surely he was hurting.

"It's not so terrible. I have my home in Los Angeles. That's where my life is," he said.

His mother asked him what he'd done with all his things.

He said, "It's all been put in storage."

"I see. Is that expensive?"

"It's not cheap."

"Hmm. But you have money now. Did you do all right?"

"I did fine," he told her.

How fine had he done? He wasn't advertising the number. Had he made more than a million?

"Around a million," he said.

"Of course, the government will take their share. Was a realtor involved?"

"Yes."

"And so the realtor will get her cut. Well, it's never as much as you think it is."

"That's true," he answered her.

"If I sold the loft, maybe I'd get six or seven. But after all was said and done, maybe I'd see four. Not that I wouldn't take it. Right now, anything would help."

"Mom, I love you," he said, "but I have to go now. I'll be home later. We'll have time to talk tomorrow. I'm here for another few days. Isn't that nice? So sleep well. I'll see you in the morning."

"You're leaving?"

"Yes, I have to go."

"Where are you going?"

"Mom, please."

"It's just a question."

"Mom, I just, I have to go."

"Remember to take your dad's shirt," she said. "Don't walk around in all that black. Not in this city."

"All right, Mom."

It was only 5:40 p.m. The sun wouldn't set for an hour. However, Ben went to bed at six so that he could rise early and begin his morning routine, and every light in the loft was off. Oliver took the stairs down to the street and taxied to his younger sister Doris's Midtown apartment. Before he was even through the front door, he was already saying how their father had completely lost his mind. There was no hope. To ask his son to give him all his money or else take away his inheritance—it was insanity.

Doris led Oliver into the living room and directed him to sit on the sofa. But Oliver collapsed onto the white bear-fur throw beside the fireplace. Long, heavy crystals occupied the hearth. Up on the mantle was a medium-sized portrait of Doris, painted by her father more than thirty-five years ago, when she was twenty-three. In the painting, she was seated on a bicycle, with her left leg stuck out at angle. A thin young woman with dark hair and a commanding gaze, in a black skirt and white sweater, red slippers. Her arms were crossed. It made Doris happy to have been seen that way by her father: deeply intelligent and strong and beautiful. She looked the same now, with the same hair, same clothes, same posture, just aged, the skin more wrinkled and spotted, the eyes heavier at the lids. She consoled her brother. She blamed Sondra.

"We were unlucky to have ever known her."

"It's true," Oliver said.

"I was thinking about the time she almost left the company," Doris said, lighting a Kent 100 and crossing her legs. "Do you remember?"

"It was back in the winter of 1976."

"No, '77," said Doris. "We were all at the loft to discuss Sondra's future at *Shout!* Mom told her she'd be a fool to leave. What would she do if she didn't work with us? How would she make money? Every year the company was getting bigger and bigger. Dad called her a pig, an entitled little bitch."

"Well, was she ever that."

"Dad gave her the truth."

"He absolutely did."

"To have had it so fucking easy."

"Yep."

"To graduate college and immediately have this great job handed to you, without having had to do anything other than ask for it."

"The suggestion of her going off to take employment some-place else was..."

"Pathetic."

"Yes," Oliver said.

"What kind of world did she imagine she'd find out there? She needed our protection."

"She stayed with us for thirty-five years...the last to official-ly quit..."

"She did nothing for the company."

"Nothing."

"Can you imagine how great it would have been without her?"

"We had a lot of fun."

"We did. But you know what I mean."

"I do. Sondra held us back."

"I'm sure you remember the *The Twains*?"

"Those four young Frenchmen?"

"Yes. With the white suits and the floppy mustaches."

"Jesus...yes," said Oliver.

"They came from Bordeaux, but every song was about the Mississippi."

"And we were both ready to sign them."

"We were."

"There was a lot of charisma there. And the songs were catchy. Then Sondra said she didn't hear a single. But what the fuck would she know about hearing a single? Did she ever hear one?"

"And those poor Frenchmen…whatever happened to them?"

"How many times did Sondra's stupid insecurities limit us? It sickens me to think about."

"And it's still happening. Look at us now. Look at me."

"She's at fault."

"She is."

"She created this situation."

"Yep."

"Mom and Dad won't ever speak to her again."

"Why would they?"

"Mom is so hurt."

"I'm proud of you, Doris. You're doing a great job with your new label. I know you'll succeed."

"It's so much work," she said. "It never ends. Sometimes I wonder how I'll find the energy to keep going day after day."

"It's in you."

"I know it is. I'm just saying I'm tired."

"We're all tired," he replied. "You should come out to Los Angeles, spend a couple of days, relax."

"No, I couldn't do that," she said, shaking her head. "I have to run my business. If I don't, who will? I have to be at it every second of the day. That's just the way it is."

"I see."

"But what about you, Oliver? What do you do out in Los Angeles?"

Oliver folded his arms. Right now he was biding his time, soon he would start his own label. A California brand of music, broader than what they had done with *Shout!* Not just rock 'n' roll, that is, but country, and hip-hop, and world. In a couple of months, once things had settled down, he'd call their old contacts on the West Coast, take the pulse of the industry, begin scouting artists. His wife's house in Malibu had so many rooms. He would run the label out of one of them.

"Do you have a name?"

"Not yet."

"It'll come. Of course, the name is the easy part. Well, you know. You've done this before."

"I have."

A moment passed in silence. Then Doris said, "I mean, I hope you know what you'd be getting yourself into. It's so much work. You've got to really want it."

"And you need capital," Oliver said. He touched his cheek to his shoulder, then smiled as if he were imagining a great personal success. In fact, he was thinking of the money his parents had given Doris to start her new label. He said, "Mom and Dad wouldn't be able to start me off. I'd have to find other investors."

"Right. You would. That's true. But you have money now, from the apartment. You could use that. And then you wouldn't be indebted to anyone."

"I suppose," Oliver said.

"The question is, do you want that kind of risk?"

"True. And there's Mom and Dad to think about, too."

"What about them?"

"Do they need my money more than I do? And then you think about how much Dad gave to *Shout!* He put us in business and kept us solvent. No chance we would have made it otherwise. But I guess I missed my window for another hand-ful, right? Two hundred thousand, no questions asked. That's not easy to find, Doris."

"I'm aware," she said. "I'll have you know I paid back every penny."

Oliver congratulated his sister. Although he didn't believe it was true. Even if she'd had the money, she wouldn't reimburse their mother and father. Doris had always taken as much as she could from their parents. Jewelry, for instance, and cash. She found opportunities to collect her inheritance in advance. She was slick about it. Oliver asked her, "Do you think about what would happen if you ever needed more capital?"

"No."

"Because Mom and Dad wouldn't have it."

"I know they wouldn't, Oliver."

"Maybe you'd just ask Sondra. After all, she's loaded."

And then, once again, the siblings were laughing. Doris got to her feet, went into the kitchen, and poured two vodka sodas. She handed her brother the drink, and they toasted to their eldest sister. What a worthless person. What a shit. But could Oliver imagine what Sondra would say if Doris asked her for money? She would probably sue her. For what?

"For making her feel bad!"

"No. No. The request afflicted her nerves. 'Oh, Your Honor, I can't work. I can't sleep. I'm sure I have one of those stress disorders.'"

"Can we kill her?"

"We could," Oliver said. "But we won't. Besides, she's al-ready dead in my book."

Oliver flew home to California. His wife, Sheila, put him right to work in the boutiques. Indeed, it was a lot for Sheila to do the inventory, advertise sales, keep an eye on the employees, make sure their books were current, and attend to payroll. Oliver told Sheila he was glad to help, even if it did mean waking up hours before he normally would and rushing off to the store on Third Street in Santa Monica to stand around and wonder what had happened to his life. The day after landing, while sorting through merchandise and making sure, as Sheila put it, the incompetence of their employees didn't reflect on the price tags of any item, Oliver began to think about what his accountant had told him. After taxes, roughly six hundred thousand would remain of the nine hundred and ten thousand.

But if I lend Dad half a million, and keep a hundred thousand for myself, and it takes more than a year for him to return the money, how will I support myself? A powerfully distracting subject—later that day, Sheila was going back through Oliver's work and found three mispriced items.

"I'm sorry, Sheila."

"I hire people to do this job, but you can't pay them enough to care. You, I expect to get things right. These are your stores, too."

"I know. I know. I'm just jet lagged. I need a couple of days to readjust."

"Well, two people called in sick!"

"I'm not complaining, Sheila."

"And I can't be at both stores at once!"

"I know. I'm sorry."

Sheila began inspecting the display case at the front, making sure everything was in its right place. She touched the stapler next to the register, inspected the mannequins in the window. Oliver had put them in their white tennis dresses first thing after opening this morning. How moronic he'd felt, suiting up those lifeless human parts while people cruised the mall and stared at him. Sheila was wearing one of the all-denim outfits that was typical of her, with the jean shorts and jean jacket, white high-tops, a red sweatband around the forehead, and black rubber bracelets on her arms. Her light eyes had a thrilled but deranged look. The blond, shoulder-length hair was fried from too many dye jobs. The boutique, like its sister-boutique in Manhattan Beach, was the size and design of a racquetball court. Racquetball was her sport. It suited her high-strung personality. She played every day. She picked up a racquet now, spinning it in her hand. She said, "Are you happy to be back?"

"I am. It was difficult being home. Selling the apartment was very emotional. I spent so many years there."

"It isn't easy getting out of an old place."

"The packing up."

"Yes, it is hard. What did you do with your things?"

Oliver pointed across the store at his wife, nodding. He was about to tell her he had given it all away. But then he thought better of it. He said, "I sold most of it to a doorman."

"That's good," Sheila said.

"The rest I gave to charity."

"Did you keep the receipt for a tax write-off?"

"Yes. I've got it somewhere," Oliver said.

"I want to have a sale next week. How's our music section coming along?"

Sheila had asked Oliver to develop one. She would section off one-fifth of the store. He would sell records, posters, T-shirts. Had he put any thought into it?

"I've had my mind on other things."

"Thanksgiving is coming," she said. "You've got to have it up and running by the day after."

Oliver said that he couldn't put time into it now. He had other pressing demands. "And, you know," he said, suddenly,

"my father needs money from the sale of the apartment. And…
and…and here you are, going on about a music section."

"What are you talking about?"

Oliver's face suddenly looked crushed. Tall yet stooped, with
his arms held out to his wife, he said, "My father…he has a
colossal debt from the lawsuit with Sondra. Almost a million
dollars."

"And he wants you to pay if off?"

"He says he's out of money."

"What about the loft?"

"He won't sell it. It's where he works."

"Where he works?"

"Yes!" Oliver snapped.

"We were going to use that money to pay off the debt from
the stores."

"I know."

"It's what we talked about, Oliver."

"I know we did."

"You promised me."

"I'm sorry, Sheila."

Her blue eyes stormy, she said, "So how much?"

"How much what?"

"How much are you going to give him?"

"I think about a…about half a million."

"Half a million!"

"And the rest we'll use to cut our debt."

"What rest? There is no rest! We'd lose the stores."

Instead of pointing out the pleasure this would give him,
Oliver said, "Sheila, my parents are more important than these
stores. I'm their son. I have to do this for them. After everything
they've given me, they deserve this. It's just what any person who
loves his parents would do. And their other children have been so

absorbed in their own lives. Doris with her new company. And then Sondra with her lawsuits. I'm all they've got. And I'm not even in New York. Well, no, no, I have to do this, Sheila. I just do."

Sheila shook her head, the expression of devastation strong through her face. She had thought that she would finally get above financial insecurity and start breathing normally again. And now? She would have to continue with that fight? Sheila smacked the head of the racquet into the floor. "I can't believe you're doing this to me!"

On the way home that evening, Oliver and Sheila stopped at the Ralph's for groceries. Sheila ushered the rickety metal cart through the aisles, propelled by debt stress, cynicism, temper. Oliver reminded his wife of her heart condition. She shouldn't get so upset. It was dangerous. The doctors had said so. Besides, couldn't they discuss something else for one minute? They'd been talking about the money all day.

"And you can't eat that," Oliver said, returning a pack of bacon to the shelf. "Or that!"

Sheila had her hand on a tube of breakfast sausage. She said, "Don't tell me what to do," and she threw it in the cart.

Oliver snatched up the meat. "You want to kill yourself?" Oliver, as awake as he'd been all day, said, "I can't be on you every minute. You have to take care of yourself."

"If my heart needs anything right now, it's half a million dollars."

"Oh, give me a break, Sheila."

"I lie awake every night thinking about that debt. I have no peace from it."

Oliver felt heat spreading through his face. He said, "We'll have to figure out another way to pay it off. That's all there is to it."

Thirty minutes later, they arrived home. Oliver said he would make dinner, that Sheila should sit outside, watch the ocean, the surfers, the clouds, the seagulls. In the kitchen, he chopped vegetables, steamed broccoli, and prepared a whole wheat rigatoni. He brought the food out to the picnic table. Sheila was lying in the hammock. Her eyes were closed. Oliver said, "Dinner's ready, sweetheart."

Sheila leaned forward and swung her feet down to the ground. She said, "We'll have to sell the house."

Though he'd yet to sit, Oliver already had his mouth full of rigatoni and he couldn't speak. Olive oil formed a shiny ring around his lips, and parmesan cheese was caught in his stubble. He swallowed then, and said, "Oh, shut up, please!"

"I'm just telling you the truth. We'll have to sell it. How else am I going to pay back the banks?"

"We'll find a way."

"I don't know if we will, Oliver."

"Just eat your dinner. It's getting cold."

"I have no appetite."

"I cooked for you!"

"And I'm not hungry!"

Sheila sulked at the picnic table. She asked her husband if he knew what it was like to be beleaguered by debt. The constant tallying up of numbers. Would she have enough to get by this month? Yes, if she sold this much. And then spent less here, and lapsed on a payment there. But what about the month after? She was nearly out of credit. The banks wouldn't offer her more cards, wouldn't extend her limits. She had gone back to them twice in the last six months. They hadn't changed their answer. She had even sought investment from friends. People with big wallets. Nothing. She was stuck with this deficit.

"Just eat your dinner."

But now Sheila was leaning into her left hand. In a matter of seconds, she had become so sweaty. She didn't like being asked if she was okay. Ever since her heart attack, Oliver had done too much of that in her opinion; she'd told him that he must stop. But he couldn't help himself now.

"Are you okay?" he said.

"Yes," she answered him, her eyes lost in fear.

"You're sure? Do you need me to call 911?"

"Uh-uh."

"Are you having a heart attack?"

"No!"

"You look like you might be."

"I'm not! Just get me a paper bag!"

Oliver ran inside to the kitchen, pulling open the cabinets under the sink, and found a paper bag. He didn't notice the hole in the bottom. And when he brought the bag to his wife, Sheila, from on her knees, said, "This one won't fucking work. It's torn. Is there another?"

"I'm calling 911!"

"No. Just get me a fucking paper bag without a hole in it! Oh, forget it, I'll do it myself."

Sheila dragged herself inside. She ransacked the cabinet beneath the sink. Ajax, Palmolive, Brillo pads—everything thrown over her shoulder and plunging to the floor. At last, a pristine brown paper bag. Sheila put it to her mouth and began breathing in and out, the bag clenching up and then ballooning from the end of her lips. Oliver stared at his wife. She was stretched across the kitchen floor. Her eyes looked caved in, her blond hair was stuck to her skin, her face drained of color. He got down on the floor beside her. He said, "I'm sorry, Sheila. I'm so sorry."

"Mmmmm."

"Are you okay?"

Sheila said she was, then she put her head in Oliver's lap and shut her eyes.

"Do you need anything? Let me get you a cold towel."

"That's okay. Just don't move," she said, clutching his leg. "Just stay right there. I'll be fine."

Despite his wife's panic attack, Oliver had five hundred thousand dollars wired into his father's account the next day. Ben called when the money went through. Oliver expected to hear a quality in his father's voice that would make amends for a lifetime of mistreatment. But Ben didn't mention the money. Eliza had suffered bleeding on the brain while at the house in Southampton the day before. Ben told his son that she had been moved to the hospital. Oliver returned directly to New York. He stayed at the loft on Wooster. He rode the LIRR back and forth through Long Island every day to be with his mother, and he reported to his father about her state. He tried to be hopeful, though the news was not good: Eliza was in a coma. Her Parkinson's was complicating matters further. He tried to keep Ben's faith up. He told him that she would pull through. That she was a fighter, he shouldn't worry, she would make it.

Today, Oliver was with his mother at the hospital, and Doris showed. But it was too painful for Eliza's youngest child to see her mother with tubes down her throat and convulsing on a bed—Doris said she couldn't stay long, fifteen minutes at most. She spent this time on the phone with her sister. She'd called Sondra from Eliza's room. She said, "You've killed your mother, and I hope you're fucking happy."

"Mommy's dead?" Sondra said.

"Almost, yes."

"You should know I'm planning an appeal. You're a criminal and deserve to be behind bars, especially after everything I've done for you and *Shout!*"

Doris began to scream, "No, no, no! Sondra, you wasted everyone's time at *Shout!* Mine, yours, everyone's. You were so far outside your element at that company. You had no fucking idea what you were doing. And now your mother is dying, and you're responsible. She's in a hospital in Long Island, and you put her here. You drowned her in grief and poisoned her body. For the rest of your life, when you open your eyes each morning, I hope you think about your mother and why you no longer have one. Go straight to the mirror and take a long look at yourself. 'I killed my mother,' you should say, 'with my stupidity, with my heartlessness, with my little insignificant life.' You'll probably end up having to do the same about your father. I doubt he'll be long for this world. He's a wreck. He can't work. All he does is worry about Mom."

Sondra was in the Range Rover, driving back from the city to Scarsdale. Her husband, Steven Katz, the doctor, was at the wheel. The phone was set to speaker. Accelerating up a snowy incline, Steven told Doris that his conscience wasn't troubled by the lawsuit. He said the same was true of his wife. "Do you think we care about Ben or Eliza? Because we don't, and we haven't for years. How they've treated us and our son is unforgivable."

But Doris wouldn't accept anyone saying anything bad about her mother or father. "Ben and Eliza have been generous with their love, loyal, supportive, nurturing of their children's minds and ambitions. If you feel that you were mistreated, it's because you didn't show them respect. That's the problem with the two of you, such arrogant pricks, you think the world should come and bow before you."

What was the fine for lighting up in a hospital? Doris didn't care. She had smoked on airplanes before, a puff in the bathroom and a spritz of No. 5 before returning to her seat. The street was eight floors down, and you had to ride the elevator with doctors, the sick and dying. Not to mention empty your pockets for security. And the weather outside was cold, the thought of which made her body stiffen. She found a single-occupancy bathroom down the hall from Eliza's room and locked herself inside. Sitting on the toilet, she rolled the wheel of the lighter under her thumb. She had stopped listening to her sister. All of a sudden, however, she said, "That you think you still deserve any of our parents' money proves you're a psycho!"

"I won't be blamed for our mother's poor health," Sondra answered. "She's had this disease for twenty years."

"But let there be no mistaking it, you did her in."

"As a doctor—"

"Shut up, please, Steven! I didn't ask your opinion. No one likes you. Just go away. Go away and sue someone else. I'll run my company and make millions, and I'll love my parents and live a productive life. You, Sondra, should get a life. Get a fucking life. Do something useful with yourself. I don't know what, but *something*."

Steven stroked his neck, his eyes full and forehead pulsating with a surge of defensive feeling for his wife. He began to recall the argument he'd had with Ben Arkin about *American Beauty*. An outstanding piece of filmmaking, he thought, what with its isolated male lead out of love with his two-timing wife having shower jerkoffs about his daughter's classmate—this was him, and the movie had brought him back from a very lonely, far-away ledge. Then for his mother-in-law's birthday, he'd gone to the Arkin loft. Looking to strike up conversation at the table, he'd mentioned the film, and the artist, with everyone feverishly awaiting his reply, had stalled, pompously scratching at his round chin, his lips meanly poised to strike the doctor, and blue eyes demonically shrinking: "Ten years ago I decided I wouldn't see Hollywood movies anymore. But I went and saw that piece of shit—suckered by the critics—and that old decision was reconfirmed. Just a very bad movie with a hundred cheap emotional hooks meant for schmucks like you, Steven, to lap up."

Oliver and Sondra had had to pull Steven off of Ben. That was the last time the doctor had seen his wife's father.

And now the film was ruined for him.

Having mentally drifted, Steven was surprised to find the steering wheel tight between all ten of his fingers, the chaotic sound of the windshield wipers, and his wife and sister-in-law still arguing on the phone. He'd told his colleague at the children's oncology wing of Mount Sinai about these zone-outs. They happened frequently. The doctor said Steven shouldn't worry, as long as he wasn't doing something that required his full attention. Well, the car was now in park, and he had put it there in advance of this episode. Regarding himself in the rearview mirror, he thought, *Good job.* He saw a man approaching sixty-five who still had a full head of hair, a great father and husband, a doctor who had helped hundreds of children beat cancer. Nevertheless, he could admit that he did find pleasure in suing his wife's family. Originally, he'd sought a strong relationship with Ben. He'd believed they would be close friends, confidantes. Mentioning this to Sondra some thirty-three years ago, she had admonished him to expect little from her father. If they could be civil during holidays, that would be an achievement.

Beyond the windows of the Range Rover, the snow was coming down heavier than in the minutes before and Steven threw the car into gear. They were only two miles from home. He would get them there safely. But if anxiety interfered with his steering, he would hand the car off to Sondra. She was still haggling with her sister. Doris wouldn't tell her which hospital Eliza had been admitted to.

"You're outrageous, Doris. If my mother is dying, I'm going to visit her. You won't keep me away."

"Get off the phone now," Steven said to her. "I can't drive like this."

Sondra pressed the phone to her shoulder. "She won't tell me where they're keeping my mother."

"I'll make a call. We'll find out. Just get off the phone."

"Not till I get what I want."

"If you don't shut up, I'm going to crash the car!"

Sondra hung up then, without another word.

Through a doctor friend, Steven learned that Eliza was at Southampton Hospital. The drive from their home in Scarsdale was two and a half hours. Sondra set out the following morning, bracing for a fight with Doris. When she got to the hospital, she didn't find Doris or her father, though. Only Oliver. Without speaking, they embraced, then settled around their ailing mother. Sondra placed her hands on Eliza's legs, not out of affection, but to stop their spastic motion. She had thought she'd find her mother in better condition. At least able to communicate. How terrible she looked. There was no coming back from here.

"None of this surprises me," said Sondra.

Oliver, who'd slept in the hospital room the night before, and would do so twenty more times in the weeks ahead, was picking up the white pillows of his makeshift bed from the floor and stacking them on the radiator at the window next to boxes of cereal bars, bananas, nuts, dried fruits, and empty cups of coffee.

"Look at her…completely annihilated by life, and by Ben. No, it doesn't surprise me." She slipped out of her mink coat, hanging it over her right arm. "I want to thank you for not bringing up the lawsuit."

"I wasn't going to."

"I just want to visit with my mother and then leave."

"Fine."

"I don't want to see Doris or Daddy."

"They don't come here. They can't bear to be in this place, to see Mom in this condition. I tell them everything that's happening and keep an eye on the doctors, the nurses, and make sure Mom's being well cared for."

Sondra closed her eyes, her head turned. She said, "And what are you after?"

"I'm sorry?"

"I mean, since I don't buy this story of you keeping a watch over Mom out of the goodness of your heart, what are you doing here?"

Oliver, fighting the urge to slug his sister, said, "I am doing what any decent child would do, and that's taking care of my sick mother. You should think a little bit about how much you've neglected your parents over the last fifteen years. It's appalling!" He left the room.

Sondra scoffed. What did her brother know about anything? Decent child? Right. But could they save this woman? It did seem like death would suit her best. And yet look how this writhing body struggled to go on. Where was this strong will coming from? Had it always been there? Sondra decided that it had, yes. Which explained how Eliza had withstood a life with Ben. But what a fool! To have accepted a despot for a husband. It made Sondra furious. Of course, back in the '60s, having moved from Queens to a palatial home on Madison and Sixty-Sixth, Sondra would sneak from her bedroom at night to see all those handsome men and fashionable women at her parents' parties. Everyone so chic. Her mother was a wonderful host. And all the men were after her. She was funny, was the thing, and calculating. And she knew everyone and their children and the schools they attended by name. Eliza had something figured out, Sondra reckoned, because Ben would hand her whole stacks of hundred-dollar bills, and up and down Madison her mother would go, buying whatever she wanted. Sometimes Sondra would tag along with her. About a dress or pair of shoes, her mother would ask, "This one or that?" then she'd leave the store with both. That was admirable.

She brought her cheek to rest against her mother. Asked if she could hear her. Well, could she? Sondra said the name Eliza twice. She tapped her mother on the hand, she touched her lips, she sidled up closer, intertwining their fingers. She apologized for having to leave so soon, she would come back to the hospital the next day. That she wouldn't have to worry about running into her father or sister made it much easier. She didn't want to sit with Oliver, either. However, he would give her space to be alone with their mother, and that was what she wanted.

But Sondra didn't return to see her mother. She would tell her husband the night before that she would be going out for a visit the following day, then get in the car, and drive as far as the end of the road, stop, and say to herself, "You have to go. You must." But then she would sit with her foot off the gas, between tall hedges, on the suburban street. And she would eventually turn back to the house. She would make the excuse that she didn't want to see her mother that way. That it didn't do anything good for anyone. So why do it? Why waste the time?

V. GET THE POLICE

Two weeks later, on a cold, clear February morning, Eliza passed away. At the cemetery the following day, and then at the loft during the shiva sitting, Doris was in a frantic state. She told Rebecca that if Sondra showed up, she would need help throwing her out. Because Sondra wasn't welcome here. There were no two ways about it. Did Rebecca understand? Could she be counted on? Rebecca asked her aunt if she or anyone had even told Sondra about her mother. Doris said that Sondra had killed her mother and, therefore, she didn't deserve to know. Killed her? Yes, Doris screamed.

Rebecca had been at the Arkin loft for seven hours. She wondered how much longer she was expected to stay. She couldn't take much more of this. Especially now, with Doris pointing across the crowded loft at her parents' bedroom door. Oliver had been asleep there since returning from the cemetery. She said, "Rebecca, listen to me please. You have to get your father out of this place. It's not his home. He doesn't have to go back to California, but he can't stay here. My mother's dead. Do me this favor and talk to him."

"My father came to town to take care of his mother and be with her at the hospital. Now give him a moment. He wants to get back to California, to his life…his regular life. This is a very difficult time for him."

"It's a difficult time for all of us."

"Yes."

"I mean, look at *my* father. I've never seen him like this. He's got to get up. Maybe he wants to eat. I'll be back. You won't leave, will you? You have to stay with me. I can't do this alone."

Doris slipped off into the crowd. Ben was lying on the pink divan at the back of the large room. His head was raised on a white pillow, a pair of black sunglasses hiding his eyes. A man of middle years came and shook his hand, speaking into the artist's ear. Rebecca could see Ben lean forward so as to hear, but his lips didn't move. The loft had never seen this many visitors. Rebecca counted more than seventy people. Ben's artwork had been moved into his studio to make space. But there wasn't the furniture to accommodate so many guests. Nearly everyone stood.

Rebecca saw Eliza's brother, Gregory, fixing himself a plate of food, and she went to him.

"Hi there." She brought her arms around his waist.

"How are you, darling?"

"I'm sorry about your sister."

Gregory thanked her. There was nothing particularly mournful about his comportment. He loathed Ben, and beneath his bald pate, he must have been privately celebrating the artist's demise. Ben was in large part responsible for Gregory's decision to practice psychiatry. Ben's abuse, his temper—a poison secreted into the minds of so many people—had pushed Gregory to the limits of his own sanity. It was only two years before, after a long hiatus, that Gregory had begun to see his sister again. Eight years earlier, he'd cut Eliza and Ben off, having decided that he wouldn't suffer any more degradation at the hands of the artist. Oh, the anger he would feel after any visit.

Ben would ignore him for the first hour. Then his brother-in-law would come from his studio, wouldn't say hello or even look Gregory's way but go straight past him, and return five minutes later with a cup of hot coffee. He would sit in a chair, drinking the coffee, not even offering his guest any but after every sip his tongue smacking against his lips, and his *ahhhhhh-hhhs*. Gregory came all the way from the East Seventies, and yet Ben wouldn't even say hello. Because he was an asshole of the highest order. And who did he think he was? God. But why did Gregory even come in the first place? Because of his sister, yes, and his desire for a relationship with her. She was eleven years his senior, though, and she should have been more protective of her younger brother. He never once heard her protest when Ben acted rudely. If she'd spoken out against his behavior, or pulled him aside and asked for patience, he would have loved her for it.

Now Gregory brought up Oliver. How was he doing?

"He'll be okay," Rebecca said.

"Where's his wife? I don't see her here."

"She isn't coming."

"Why not?"

"I don't know."

"But they're still married, aren't they?"

"Yes."

Not satisfied with Rebecca's answer, Gregory said, "I hear she's been in California all this time, and that your father's been at the loft."

"That's right."

"But they're still married?"

"Yes," Rebecca repeated.

Gregory did look happy now, his blue eyes big and jovial, his chest puffed out. He wore a white beard, Freud-like. His body was lean. He had a red, freckled complexion. He kept his cell phone locked into a clip on his belt. "And are Doris and your father getting along?"

"I don't know anything," she told him. "My father keeps me in the dark. He doesn't want to involve me in his affairs. I don't ask questions."

Gregory said, "You know, when my mother died, you'll maybe remember, it was all-out warfare. My sister and our siblings, everyone wanted everything, every last coaster and napkin ring. Things which hadn't meant anything to us for the past fifty years as we came and went from our parents' home suddenly had great meaning. It took me time to come to the point where I am now. But I can say that I too could have acted better. I don't even speak to my older brothers and sisters these days. I'm sure you heard that my brother, Tom, and I had a row, and Tom broke my tooth." Gregory drew back his cheek, pointing at a molar. "Cost six thousand to fix. And do you know what we were fighting about? A box of photos. Photos neither of us had seen for more than thirty years. Well, don't be surprised if your father and his sisters have a difficult time ahead. There's a lot to divvy up, not all of which will necessarily be spelled out in the will."

Rebecca shrugged at her uncle. "Nothing gets divvied yet. Ben's still alive."

"But he won't be forever." Gregory was stern. "And you're your father's daughter. And if what happens with Ben and Eliza is anything like what happened with my parents, all the grandchildren will get involved. People take sides, is what I'm saying. Cousins that you've felt close to your whole life might not show up at holiday dinners anymore. Might not even call to tell you they can't make it. Sondra's one example. She came to my mother's home the day we were going through her things.

I didn't know what she was doing there. I'm not sure how she found out we were going to be there. But she started telling us that my mother had promised her the salt and pepper shakers. My sister, Elaine, was not for letting Sondra have them. Which upset Eliza. She asked what it mattered if Sondra had the salt and pepper shakers. Everyone knew Sondra collected salt and pepper shakers, and it didn't seem odd that my mother would've said Sondra could have hers. So just let her have the salt and pepper shakers, right? But Elaine said no. Because *she* wanted them. Elaine got loud, and it looked like she might hit Eliza. Then Sondra shoved Elaine. Elaine tried to retaliate, and my brothers and I had to separate the women. This was all in the first ten minutes of being at the house. An hour later, Tom and I were wrestling on the lawn. We had to bring in a woman who specialized in resolving these kinds of disputes. It was too emotional to deal with on our own."

"I refuse to worry about what hasn't happened yet," said Rebecca.

"That's good, but—"

"The will is going to clarify everything."

"That would be best, yes."

"Eliza just died, Gregory. I don't think it's right to talk about this sort of thing. Let's stop, please."

"Okay. I'm sorry. We don't have to."

"Thank you, Gregory."

Over the next three months, Ben hardly moved. To see him mute and powerless was a shock to anyone who had known him. Rebecca visited one afternoon, and she couldn't believe his condition. At first, she thought he was dead. Then he let out a moan. Oliver had been with his father all this time. He said that Ben was sleeping twenty-two hours a day. He went to the bathroom in a pot, which Oliver helped him to use. The divan where Ben lay was surrounded by pill bottles and used towels.

Rebecca sat down next to her grandfather on a metal folding chair. She took his hand. Only when shaking hello and good-bye had she ever held his hand in the past—Ben did not hug, he was not the kind to invite his grandchild up onto his lap, he did not let Rebecca call him Grandpa, Ben would do. Or Ark.

Now she rubbed his fingers.

"That's great," Oliver was saying. "Massage him. Get the life going in his hands. Come on, Dad. You're going to paint again."

"Dad, please," Rebecca said. "He can't hear you."

"Yes, he can!" Oliver cried. "I spend my days talking to him, just like I did with my mother. They hear you. You might not think it. But they do."

"Dad, even if that's true, you shouldn't be here. Ben has a nurse. She can do everything for him. You have to go back to L.A."

"I won't leave him, Rebecca. Don't you know you can't trust these nurses? They don't give the right care. They're not attentive. I'm telling you, they'll let you sit in your shit for an hour. They won't move you around, and you'll get bedsores. They have no idea when you're thirsty, or if you need your pillow adjusted. No, I have to make sure that things get done the way they're supposed to, or your grandfather will suffer. That's my job now."

She wouldn't push her father's emotions any further. Instead, she said, "I'll shave Ben's face. He needs it."

Minutes later, Rebecca returned from the bathroom with a razor, shaving cream, a bowl of hot water, and a towel. Oliver was pulling his father up to sit. Ben, with closed eyes and a limp body, whimpered in his bathrobe. Rebecca began to lather her grandfather's face with shaving cream. She brought the razor through the bowl of hot water. The hairs were soft and came up easily. Her grandfather was silent and still. Rebecca was careful with the razor around Ben's neck, where the skin folded in on itself and had to be pulled back to get at the hairs. Rebecca worked briskly over this part. Ran the blade through the water and saw her father kiss Ben's head. Shaving Ben's mustache, she spread her fingers over his mouth, stretching the skin, and was eager to be done with it. She didn't bother to get every hair below his nostrils. In between strokes of the razor, she watched Ben's eyes to make sure they remained closed. What would he think if he awoke and found her leaning over him? Would he know her? Would he understand where he was? Either way, her father was pleased.

That weekend, Oliver asked his daughter to go to Southampton. They would take her grandfather. What Ben needed was a change of scenery. The beach. Could she make the time? He couldn't do it alone. It was too hard for him to lift his father. Yes, getting Ben up off the divan, out of the loft, into the car and the rest of it was more than he could handle on his own. She could take her work with her, sit at the head of the dining table just like her grandfather had every weekend for the last thirty years, and do it there. He could really use her company, too. And he didn't drive. Rebecca suggested, in that case, her father call up Jerome. He would take them. But Oliver said that was out of the question. He wouldn't spend all that time with his father's assistant, he required a certain level of privacy, his mother had passed and he didn't want to go through all his feelings in front of a stranger.

And so Rebecca went to Southampton. She did the driving and helped her father with Ben. But most of the time, she worked. Occupying Ben's seat at the dining table, while her grandfather slept in a wheelchair on the deck, caused her mind to wander and stall. She watched him through the large sliding-glass doors, his head hung forward, his mouth open, and saliva dripping from his lips. Her father had brought Ben's last bag of reading materials, his cups of blue and red pens, his journals. He set it all out for the artist on the patio table under the umbrella. Of course, Ben didn't touch any of it. But the wind made a mess of things, the newspaper clippings ending up in the swimming pool and in the woods beyond the deck. Meanwhile, her father stayed intensely busy. He cleaned and baked and even gave the front steps of the house a new coat of white paint. He had hardly said a word to Rebecca all weekend. Well, it was just two days and two nights, she reckoned. She could do it. At least this once.

When she dropped her father and grandfather at the loft that Sunday afternoon, however, Oliver said they should go back to Southampton the following weekend. That he had had a wonderful time. Should they meet right back here on Friday at 5 p.m.? Yes? Okay, good. He and her grandfather would be ready then.

On Wednesday evening, Rebecca was at the firm, reading through documents. It was almost midnight. How long had she been at the office? If she spent too many hours in her chair, some part of her back would slip out of place, her neck would tighten and lock, a nerve would get pinched. She had to circulate the blood by taking a spin around the office floor, or her mind would become hazy and she would have to redo her work.

Even ten years into the job, she hadn't grown accustomed to the night-empty halls. The overhead lights were on, the office doors shut. The cubicles at the middle where the paralegals and secretaries sat were vacated. Was there anyone here? Usually someone was tucked away in some office. She would see a body curled up on the floor. Or just hear a door slam. But now Rebecca's cell phone was ringing. No one called her this late. It was Julia Raines. She was an intimate friend of the Arkin family, a one-time schoolmate of Doris's. She would come with her husband and daughter to Thanksgiving, and had even organized Ben and Eliza's fiftieth wedding anniversary. But she had never called Rebecca before. And now she was saying that Ben had gone unconscious yesterday evening. He'd been brought to the hospital. Oliver had been with him. Doris, too. It was pneumonia.

"Rebecca, he received top care. I'm sorry. They were unable to save him."

Julia continued to speak. She was very good at breaking bad news. She knew just what people wanted to hear, how to say it. Julia's voice, indicative of her whole body—the wide hips and large bosom, the long black hair and dark brow—had a propensity for the low end. In that deep register, she told Rebecca how she'd been with Oliver all day at the hospital. He was coping. She had brought him back to the loft an hour before, and taken the liberty of arranging for Rebecca to transport him to the cemetery for Ben's funeral, which would be held the following day.

"All right?"

"Yes."

"You don't have to call him now. After the day he's had, I'm sure he's asleep."

"Okay, Julia."

"Show up tomorrow at nine outside the loft, with the Cadillac. Your father will be there."

Rebecca did as Julia had instructed, arriving at the loft the next morning in her grandfather's car. From the moment Oliver stepped out onto the sidewalk, through all the exits in Queens, the scenery along the black road changing from city to suburb, he was on the phone with his wife, insisting that he was fine, that there was nothing to worry about. Sheila didn't have to fly in, no. He had Rebecca here. She was taking good care of him.

Ben had told his granddaughter more than once that he wanted to be cremated and to have his ashes scattered along the beach in Southampton. But Eliza had made him agree to this place, which was not Ben—the crisp green grass, the hedges perfectly manicured, the large black gates at the entrance. The service was at ten sharp. They'd been told to be on time. The rabbi had to get on to other funerals, and he wouldn't wait. Twenty minutes before the funeral was set to begin, they parked the car. Rebecca opened a black umbrella, giving her father cover from the hot May sun. Walking toward the excavated earth where Ben would soon be interred, she saw that Oliver no longer filled out his black suit, his body slimmed by crisis. The jacket could have used a pressing. Rebecca said, "Do you need anything, Dad?"

"No."

"I have a bottle of water if you're thirsty."

Oliver didn't reply. His face was sunken, damp. Rebecca gave her father's arm a tug, said, "Look, Dad. It's Emma."

For an instant Oliver's cheeks regained some of the color they'd lost over the past months from being indoors, nursing his parents. "Oh thank God," he said, and marched off in Emma's direction, leaving his daughter alone.

Thirty paces away, in the shade of a mausoleum, Rebecca could see Laura Saks, her father's ex-fiancée. How had she found out about the service? Why had she come? Her father had been engaged to Laura three times. As much as anyone, Rebecca had expected them to marry. Rebecca had been pleased that they hadn't. More than the mold growing in the floorboards under

Oliver's bed, her father had been allergic to this woman. In the last years of their relationship, Laura had been responsible for hundreds of Oliver's headaches, stomach bugs, dizzy spells, and muscle spasms. What person could make another so sick, and at the same time remain attractive? But Laura and her father didn't speak anymore. So then what was she doing here?

"Rebecca. Rebecca, hi."

Rebecca turned around and started. Her cousin Marcus was coming straight for her. He was Sondra's child, and Rebecca began looking out across the cemetery, concerned that her father's sister was here. Now, to break the tension, she thought of saying a kind word to her cousin. Did he feel it, too? He must.

"Nice to see you," she told Marcus.

"Same to you," he said. He looked like a young Freewheelin' Bob Dylan, with the light curly hair and sensitive eyes. He nodded heavily, his gaze overbearing. "And you're doing all right?" he asked.

"Pretty well," Rebecca said. She didn't feel any desire to share her thoughts with him.

"I've worried about this day my entire life. You too, I'm sure."

Rebecca couldn't help but answer yes.

"My mother, your father, Doris—have you ever known a more dysfunctional group?"

"No, I don't think so."

"I've always looked ahead to Ben's death with fear. Like, the only thing keeping our parents and our aunt from tearing off each other's heads were their parents, and now there's no one to police them."

"I haven't been thinking about it."

"No?"

"No, Marcus."

"How can you *not* think about it?"

"I just don't, Marcus."

"What about your dad?"

"What about him?"

"Is he all right?"

"Yes. He's fine."

"Have I offended you?"

"No. I'm sorry, Marcus. I won't get into it now."

Rebecca crossed the dark green lawn. She could feel the heat radiating up from the grass. Her heels sunk into the earth, and she moved weight into the toe of her shoe. She didn't mean to reject her cousin. Why, she'd heard all the sense he'd just been making. She knew his intentions were good. But she couldn't afford him her energy at this moment. She had none to spare.

Now, in a patch of gravestones laid flat against the ground in an even grid, Rebecca was within earshot of her father and Emma. She heard Oliver speak to his friend of how he was worn out by death. And that for the first time he had no home in New York City. He said he and his wife were out of money, and that he'd lent his father half a million, and was waiting to get it back, as well as the house in Southampton, which Eliza had promised him.

"I can't leave New York until I get it all."

Emma was a thin, blond ex-New Yorker now residing in Raleigh. Her gray-blue eyes were not the same shape. She was short and sturdy, athletic. She asked Oliver, "Can you stand being in the loft?"

"No," he said. "It's not good for me there."

"Where would you like to be?"

"In my old apartment," he said. "If I'd known I was going to be spending all this time in New York, I never would have sold it."

"Do you really feel that way, Dad?" Rebecca asked.

"Yes, Rebecca. Look at me. I'm homeless."

"You're not homeless."

"But I am."

"No, you are not," Rebecca said.

"Call it what you will, but I have no home!" Oliver shouted.

Emma's worried gaze locked on Oliver. Her cheeks were redder. In a quiet voice, she said she had a thought. Her father lived on West Eighty-Eighth Street and Riverside in the large apartment in which she'd been raised, and where she and Oliver had played as children. Bruce Barry was eighty-two but with it, a heavy socializer, a card player. He lived alone in the apartment, refusing a nurse. He still did fifty pushups a day, fifty crunches, did his own grocery shopping, and got himself to and from doctor appointments. But Emma worried about him. What if he were to hurt himself? Who would help him? Her point was that she would like it if someone were there in the apartment. Perhaps Oliver could take one of the four vacant bedrooms and live for free.

"I love your father," Oliver said. "I've always loved him."

"I would have to ask him first," Emma cautioned. "But I don't see him saying no. He's always liked you, too. He'd enjoy having you around."

Rebecca put up a hand in protest. For her father to live with an old man and serve in the role of nurse—no matter in how limited a capacity—was out of the question. She said, "You've spent the past four months taking care of your mother and father, Dad. I will give you money to rent an apartment before that happens. Thank you, Emma. But my father needs to start spending some more time with people his own age."

Emma, feeling her friend's predicament very keenly now, said, "Of course. It was just a suggestion."

"You know, my daughter makes big bucks," Oliver said.

"Dad, please."

"What?" Oliver didn't realize that he was screaming. "I'm proud to be able to say that. I never made money like you. She could put me up at the Plaza for a month, no problem."

"The mortgage payments eat up everything I have," Rebecca told Emma. "Things always feel tight."

"She takes me out to the priciest restaurants."

"Dad, stop."

"But it's true. She'll make partner one day soon. She'll be rich."

"Not true," Rebecca said, to Emma.

"Oliver! Oliver!" Laura Saks, that bone-thin woman with the small, brittle nose, dark, penetrating eyes, and long wavy hair was walking right at them. She wasn't more than twenty feet away now. Perhaps she thought a big smile would make up for the fact that she didn't belong here.

Rebecca put her hand directly on her father's chest. "Did you invite Laura?"

"I don't remember."

"You don't remember?"

"I don't know."

"Dad, did you or didn't you?"

"No. I didn't."

Rebecca searched his eyes for truth. "She's out of her mind, and she's obsessed with you."

"Just be nice!"

However, all at once, the attention moved off Laura. For Doris was approaching the gravesite, with Julia Raines a step behind her. Doris saw Sondra at the grave, and the youngest Arkin daughter immediately had a fit. She screamed, in her tight black strapless dress, among the group of mourners, that Sondra could not be here.

"You better leave!"

Marcus, standing in front of his mother, said, "She has as much a right to be here as anyone. And she will pay her respects."

Doris said, "Shut up, you know-it-all twerp."

"Do not talk to my son that way!" shouted Sondra.

"My grandfather is dead," Marcus said. With his dimpled chin and the broad forehead, the upper half of his face so clearly resembled Ben's. He said, "I loved him. My mother loved him too."

"That's just fucking bullshit," said Doris, turning to Rebecca for support.

The rabbi stepped forward with one arthritic hand lifted in the air. His gray beard was spotty, except at the mustache, which curled downward at the ends. His yarmulke, covering a bald head, was black, his eyeglasses gold wire-framed. He began to say, "Sons and daughters, sons and daughters, please be quiet. This is not the time for argument. Be quiet. Everyone quiet."

"She sued her parents and me and her brother." Julia's hands held Doris at the shoulders, and she was telling her to be calm.

"That," said the rabbi, "is not important now. A man is dead. It is our job to bury him properly."

"That's not going to be possible with her here!" Doris interjected.

"Screw you," Sondra flailed.

"Fuck off!" said Doris.

"I'll kill you!"

The rabbi said, "You must honor your parent."

"Neither one of them ever could," said Oliver, in a hushed voice.

Then Doris went, "Hah! Yes."

She had spotted a police car with two officers seated inside it near the black gates of the cemetery. She was walking straight toward the vehicle, her determined steps pounding the grass. Everyone watched. Where was she going? Emma asked. What was happening now? Doris was talking to the officers. Then they got out of their car, and were now following Doris back to Ben's gravesite. The officers quietly wished the mourners their condolences. They nodded at the rabbi.

"That woman," Doris shouted, "that woman is not allowed at this funeral and should be removed from the premises."

They were short, stocky men. They squinted under their hats, the sun strong above them. "Has a restraining order been issued?"

Doris, with her hands on her hips and her shoulders turned inward, said, "Yes, a restraining order has been issued." But after a moment she changed her answer. She said, "I mean, no. No, not exactly."

The police explained to her that nothing could be done, then.

Sondra said, "Can she be arrested for making a false arrest?"

"Afraid not," said one of the officers. "We wish you all a good day."

The policemen left, and, for a moment, no one moved or spoke. The rabbi lifted the small prayer book in his hand and asked if he could continue. But then, Doris was, all of a sudden, sprinting across her father's plot. She dove at Sondra. Sondra tumbled backwards into the dirt under her sister's weight. Releasing a violent shriek that carried far across the cemetery, Doris pulled Sondra's hair, her knees locked tightly around her sister's wide hips. "I'll kill you. I'll kill you. I'll kill you," she said.

But Sondra, thick-armed and strong, delivered a blow to her sister's jaw, popping back her head. She connected a second time, and a third. Doris, her bloody lips quivering, her swelling eyes wet with tears, was at once screaming for Sondra to get off her. Marcus and Oliver and his ex-fiancée, Laura Saks, all tried pulling them apart.

Oliver cried, "Stop, Sondra. You're hurting her, stop!"

Yet the older sister would not let go. Her nails were sunk into Doris's neck. She had Doris's nose in the other hand and was twisting it. The sisters' feet, searching for leverage, kicked at the ground where Eliza's parents, Ruth and Karl, were buried. At last, they were separated.

"You fucking cunt," Doris whimpered. Julia had her in her arms. "I'll kill you. You don't deserve this life. How could you come here and ruin this day for me! This was my father's funeral. How could you!" Weeping, she fell to her knees.

Sondra stood with her head dropped forward between her shoulders, heaving. She said, "You will pay for this. I am going to the law. There are witnesses. You attacked me. I will put you in jail. I will make sure you get the highest penalty."

"You attacked me!"

"Oh, right. Sure I did. You're going to rot in prison," Sondra replied.

The rabbi began to read the kaddish. Sondra and Doris continued screaming at one another. Rebecca saw her father close his eyes. He was searching for a place to hide, thought Rebecca. He believed that he didn't belong among his siblings, that he wasn't one of those for whom conflict and chaos were the stuff of life.

The funeral ended just moments later, with a dump truck pushing dirt into Ben's grave.

VI. IT'S ALL GONE

Rebecca said: "Jerome, old friend, you missed the funeral. How's it been for you? I know this must be hard. Are you okay?"

They were in Jerome's black two-door Civic, tucked away on a quiet dead-end street in Tudor City where only a dry cleaner and a deli interrupted the strictly residential quarter. Straight above, where the surrounding tall brown brick buildings quit rising, a clear sky was visible. No one walked the sidewalks, save for a doorman in a gray uniform who was hosing down the concrete.

Jerome shut off the car engine, but at the next moment, a black sedan with powder-blue diplomatic plates pulled in behind them, honking. They were in a restricted spot. Jerome turned the car on again and rolled the car forward, making room for an ambassador. His wide neck stiffened, and he pushed out his chest. He said he had wanted to be at the service, but he'd been too sad to go, he missed Ben, it hurt so much.

Rebecca lowered her head and folded her hands in her lap, wondering why she felt nothing. Even now, with Jerome telling her how Ben had loved her and talked about her all the time, that he was proud, that he always used her as an example. "Rebecca has her head on straight. Rebecca's smart as hell."

She grinned. "What you mean is that he used me to put you down."

"Pretty much."

"Sometimes I think I became a lawyer because of him. You know, when I was a kid, and the idea came to me, I asked him what he thought, and he hugged me."

"Strange."

"It was, Jerome. But now I know why he came on so strong. He was probably thinking, be a lawyer. As a lawyer, the chances that someone will screw you are less. Because people will always try and screw you. *Everyone* is looking to screw you."

"Sounds like him."

"Your friends, your family, there's everyone to be suspicious of, to expect the worst of. So, be a lawyer, and when the time comes when that someone tries to screw you, you won't need to rely on anyone else for protection."

"Feel like I'm talking to him right now."

"Because even your lawyer is trying to screw you. You must be the primary representative of your own interests. And as the client of a lawyer, you are not *that*, and you will ultimately be screwed. See legal bill."

Jerome was shaking his head, a smile teetered on his lips. Then he looked up at Rebecca. "Can I ask you something?"

"Of course. What is it?"

"Do you ever think about refrigerators?"

"Refrigerators?" Rebecca thought Jerome was making a joke. But he said, "Yes. Refrigerators. Ben spent a lot of time thinking about them toward the end of his life. He bought eight General Electrics at the Salvation Army right before Eliza died. They're in his studio."

"Are you asking me if you should throw them away?"

Jerome said, "No. I'm not."

"So what, then?"

"They're part of Ben's final masterpiece. *The Refrigerated Library*, that's the title. I want to get into the loft and finish working on it."

"Why would you do that?"

"Because I have to."

"Right."

"I mean it, Rebecca. Ask your father or your aunt if I can spend some time at the loft."

"They'll never go for it."

"They might."

But Rebecca shook her head. She told him her father had been asleep in the loft for the last week. Ever since Ben's death, she had been riding down to Wooster in a taxi at night and looking in on him. She would find Oliver asleep in bed. She would tidy up the kitchen, put tulips in a vase by the bed, and stock the refrigerator with prepared foods. The next day, she would see how none of the tuna or egg salad or fruit had been touched. Had he eaten at all? She had wondered how long she could let him go on like this. Another week? Another two? What if a month passed, and he continued to spend every day in this dark room, asleep and disconnected from people? What would she do then?

"I can't ask this person if you can go into the loft and work on his father's art."

"What about Doris?"

"What about her?"

"Talk to her for me, please."

"What can she do? It's my father who's at the loft."

Jerome began to plead. He needed to do this. It was so important, for his mourning.

At that, Rebecca smarted. She brought her hands up over her cheeks and said, "Drive me back to work. I don't want to talk about this anymore."

Later that day, Rebecca began to think that she would talk to Doris after all. Not about Jerome, but about her father. It was difficult to know if he was in danger. She didn't consider herself a good judge. But she couldn't just let him waste away inside the loft. She had to do something.

After work, she grabbed a cab to her aunt's apartment. Doris lived on Fifty-Ninth Street, near the entrance to the Queensboro Bridge, an intersection as loud and frantic as any in the city. Upstairs, she found her aunt on a business call. A cigarette burned between Doris's lips, and she embraced her niece with one arm, saying into the phone, "No, because I need you to do it now! No, the order has to get out to the stores tomorrow morning. Yes. Yes! *Yes!* In the morning. No, I can't call and tell them they won't have it. So you figure it out. Get it done, Gordon. Bring in whoever you have to, and make it fucking happen. No, Gordon! No."

Doris turned the phone at an angle from her ear, and said, "I'm sorry, but this idiot..." Then she disappeared down a hall into a bedroom. Two young interns sat at the back of the living room, nervous little things. They watched Rebecca move about the room, following her closely with deferential eyes. Rebecca didn't introduce herself, her attention taken in at once by a large white neon sign above Doris's desk: *Doris Arkin Shouts!* On the desk was a framed photo of Doris kissing her father on the cheek. Ben was making an expression of extreme irritation.

Doris emerged from the bedroom then, her long black hair disheveled and cigarette blooming smoke. She began to apologize. They said hello again, Doris bummed Rebecca a cigarette, and they went into the kitchen—a room of a thousand white tiles and brightly polished silver piping—and milled at a large window, smoking. The ashtray was a duck with a saucer between its wings. Doris emptied it into a trash can and replaced it on the granite counter. She said, "Rebecca, I've stopped sleeping. At all hours I'm at my desk, working. I try not to think about the fact that my parents are gone, or that the lawyers from the suit with Sondra are still owed so much money. Work is the best thing for me right now. I just work and work and work."

Rebecca said, "I'm glad you have your work then, Doris. In times like these, work can be a welcome distraction."

"Your father won't help me get our parents' estate in order. I can't even get him on the phone. I love him, but he's a mess."

Something inside Rebecca's chest seemed to flip. She said, "He's not doing well."

"Rebecca, he's always been this way. I mean, I ran *Shout!* I did everything for the company. I carried my brother and sister all those years."

"Over the course of thirty-five years, I'm sure each of you had a chance to lead."

"Yes. Maybe. Your father was once…good," Doris said. "But then his heart went out of it back in the mid-eighties. As for Sondra, I don't know why she got involved in the business in the first place. She doesn't have a creative bone in her body. She has no business savvy. She didn't bring anything to *Shout!* but an inferiority complex."

"Well, I don't know about Sondra," Rebecca said. "But my father started that label. It was his idea, his interest in music that made it happen in the beginning, and over the first fifteen years he was as smart as anyone. His tastes, his instincts, they were spot on. But then my parents' divorce killed his spirit. He stopped caring about his work. It became just a job. He was miserable. In times of depression, some people shut down."

"I don't," she said.

"I know you don't, but my father does. Maybe you'll remember that at the time of his divorce, your parents were calling him every day and telling him to get it together. They harassed him. The people who should have been helping him most were making it harder and harder for him. Your sister, Sondra, did you know that she and her husband, Steven, threatened to have me taken away from my father? Taken where, I don't know… maybe to live with them. A truly frightening thought, considering that they're out of their fucking minds. But Sondra and her husband didn't think my father was fit to care for me."

"Is that so?"

"Yes," Rebecca said. "They came up to the apartment on Eightieth one night. I remember my father in his bedroom. They said they were going to take me. And whatever my dad could get his hands on, he was throwing…lamps and chairs, clothes. Eventually I was sent out with the babysitter to get ice cream. It was past my bedtime. A navy coat over my pajamas, I left the building, and went up the street to the deli. Returning to the apartment, I was stopped at the corner by the sitter. An ambulance was parked at the curb in front of the building. From fifty paces away, I saw my father was strapped down to a gurney, being wheeled into the ambulance. And I remember thinking, Don't let it be him. Please, God, don't let it be him. My dad spent three weeks at Bellevue, resting, seeing psychiatrists. I visited him there. My mother brought me. We were allowed to see him for a few minutes only. He couldn't even speak, he was so medicated." Rebecca took another of her aunt's cigarettes and lit it at the stove. She said, "But my point is this: If my father's family were made up of the kind of people who said things like, 'We're here for you. Whatever you need,' he would have stood up sooner in the aftermath of his divorce.

Instead, Ben rang at 6 a.m. and screamed at him to get up, shower, brush it off, move on. He had a sister and brother-in-law who told him they would take his child from him. All while he needed people to treat him with love and to grant him the time away to recover."

Doris said, "But even after all of that, your father just remained in bed, Rebecca. We had a company to run. You know, in the real world, a person can't simply drop out. No matter how troubled, a person has to show up and attend to responsibilities. That's the way life is."

"You're right," Rebecca replied. "You're right that in most cases a person can't just cut out because he's severely depressed. But when you own the company, and your sisters own the company, and your parents own the company, then you can take a minute to recover, because those people are loving enough to work a little harder and step up for you."

Doris had nothing to say about this. She threw her hands in the air. "But why is he still at the loft?"

"I don't know," Rebecca said.

"He can't be there."

"I know."

Doris exhaled deeply. Suddenly, a look of pleasure flashed across her face. She said, "That was some scene at the funeral, huh? They should have thrown Sondra in that cop car. I would have loved that."

Rebecca said, "Yeah," though her whole body seemed to rebel in doing so.

One of the interns came into the kitchen then. She said, "Sorry to interrupt. Margaret's on the line."

"Can't you see I'm busy? Tell Margaret I'll call her back." Doris shook her head at Rebecca. "I'm sorry. What were we talking about? Oh yes…your father."

Doris said it was ignorant to assume that Oliver would just all of a sudden break out of his state. He was in a downfall, to be sure. Rebecca had to pull him out of it before he worsened.

"What do you suggest?"

Doris took her niece's hands. She said, "Go to the loft tomorrow, throw his clothes in a suitcase, and fly him home to L.A. yourself. I mean it, you'll have to get on that plane with him, Rebecca."

"I should get on the plane with my dad?"

"Yes."

"And fly with him?"

"That's right, Rebecca. If you want to get him back home and out of this rut, it's the only way."

"You think so?"

"Get him home to his wife and let her help him take the next step."

"What if he says no?"

"He won't. Not if you're firm with him."

The next day, Rebecca returned to the loft. In fact, she had bought her father a plane ticket for 4 p.m. that afternoon. She wouldn't travel with him to Los Angeles. No—she would go to the airport, they would eat together in the terminal, she'd walk him up to security, tell him how brave he was and that she would come visit soon, and that she loved him. He'd have to get himself on the plane.

Fortunately, this morning, she found her father awake for the first time in a month. He was on the phone with Sheila. The television remained the only light in the room, and Rebecca switched on a lamp on the side table. She could hear Sheila screaming through the phone. Perhaps she was telling her husband to come home.

To give her father privacy, Rebecca went into her grandparents' walk-in closet. Nothing had been moved. Eliza's dresses hung on a rod, grouped by color. Her shoes, and shirts, and coats, and belts, and hats, great old stuff—Rebecca would like to take it all. Doris probably had everything inventoried. She would want to know why it had gone missing.

Rebecca returned from the closet into the bedroom. Oliver was still quietly listening to his wife, gazing out over large splayed feet. Then suddenly he was off. He began squinting in such a way, as if his facial muscles were working to wring out all the emotion inside him. Now he came up on his knees in the bed. His eyes were bloodshot. There was a cut on the palm of his hand, about three inches long. How had he done this? He could use a shave. Rebecca could smell his strong, musky odor. Oliver grabbed one of the used tissues in the bed—they were everywhere—and blew his nose, then threw the tissue on the floor. His arms were in motion, his head, too. He wanted to say something.

"Do you need water, Dad?"

"Yes," he said.

Even in the pitch dark, Rebecca could find a glass in the kitchen cupboard, and she filled it at the sink. She shut off the water and thought, *I have to take control. He's losing his mind.*

Back in the bedroom, her father took the glass with two hands, as if he would drop it if he didn't use both, guzzled the water down, then used the covers to wipe his face. Rebecca asked him if he would like her to cook him dinner

But then, all of a sudden, Oliver was saying how three nights ago he had been in Ben's office, looking through his father's things: journals, scraps, and other odd notes. There were so many papers in the room. Well, she knew how Ben was. Never threw away anything.

"Yes. Okay," Rebecca said.

Oliver was scratching his face, grimacing. He said he had come across a small blue shoe box, opened it for no particular reason, and found inside it a note written in Doris's handwriting to the lawyers who'd represented the family in the suit against Sondra.

"Oh," said Rebecca. "What was it?"

Again, Oliver went silent. His body shook. Such a big man, his trembling frightened Rebecca. She didn't know what to do. Get him more water, maybe? She held the glass in the air. But now she heard her father say how he had picked up this letter, and he had felt a shock. Yes, a shock, he said. And he had known at once that he'd been holding something terribly important in his hands.

"Rebecca, the paper said: 'If you want to see the remaining seven hundred and forty thousand dollars you're owed, we have to restructure my parents' will. We'll fire Mary Goldstein,' my parents' estate lawyer forever, 'and you'll take her place, and make a change whereby the house in Southampton will go, not to Oliver, but to me. I will sell the house and pay you with that money. My dad is on board. My mother needs work. We will make this happen.' Then there was a second note: 'My mother is going to sign.' And then a third note thanking the lawyers for their work on the new wills, which are all there, signed by Eliza and Ben, as well as Violet and Jerome as their witnesses. There were additional documents, including multiple copies of the old will where the house in Southampton goes to me. There was nothing about Ben repaying the money I'd lent him. Not a single word!"

"Dad, how is this possible?"

"Because Doris is a sick fucking bitch!"

"She's not capable of this."

"Yes!" Oliver screamed.

"I don't believe it."

"Well, you can go into Ben's office. All of the papers are right there on his desk. Read it for yourself."

But to go and look now was out of the question. Any show of doubt would wound her father. She said, "Dad, I don't know what to make of this, but I have to get you out of here. You have to leave this place. I bought you a ticket to L.A."

"I'm going to sue the fucking shit out of her, Rebecca!"

"Dad!"

"I'm going to make sure she burns! Mark my words."

"Dad, please. You have to calm down."

But Oliver continued screaming about his sister. She was a con artist, a criminal. He had always known that she would one day stab him in the back. Because a person knows, he kept saying. A person knows and blinds himself all the while from the obvious. Doesn't want to see. Doesn't want to believe. But it didn't take much seeing or believing to identify this kind of evil. Except that she was his sister! he cried. His sister, who he loved, and had built a career beside, and had nurtured as a child. How could she have done this to him? How could she have betrayed him? How? Had it been easy for her? Had she even had to think before acting? Had she stopped for one moment and considered that she would be ending their relationship, permanently?

Oliver cupped his hands around his daughter's face. Their eyes met. He gave her a look of the utmost gravity. He said Doris would come after her. Just wait. She would try to pull her to her side. And Rebecca had to realize that every word Doris spoke, every smile, every laugh, every touch, every gift, every invitation to a drink, dinner—it would all be part of an act that aimed to turn Rebecca against her father.

"Dad, I can't be turned against you."

But Rebecca underestimated his sister's power, he said. "She's a sociopath. You understand that, right? You do? Tell me if you don't. Because you have to know. Or else you're likely to get fucked by her too somehow."

"Yes, I understand, Dad."

"You do?"

"Yes, Dad."

Her cheeks white and eyes burning, Rebecca followed after her father. He was only wearing underwear. Some clothes would have made him seem halfway sane. He went into Ben's office, turned on the lights. There were the papers scattered everywhere across Ben's desk. New wills, old wills, handwritten notes, printed emails. Oliver said he had all the evidence right there. Everything to prove Doris had broken the law.

"Well, call her up and confront her."

"No way, Rebecca!"

"Why not?"

"No! I won't do it."

Rebecca told her father that they could talk this through. This was a misunderstanding. These wills on the table—who knew if they were copies of Ben and Eliza's actual wills. There was no reason to jump to any conclusions. "Just call her up."

"What do you think she'll say? She'll just lie to me, Rebecca. Tell me she has no idea about any of it."

"You don't know that."

"Of course, I do. I know. I know just how she is."

Rebecca looked around Ben's office. She saw his journals on a shelf. The room smelled of camphor. She said, "You have to get out of this place. I'm taking you to Los Angeles."

Oliver crumbled against Ben's desk, breathing heavily, going to pieces. He said, "I'm not going anywhere. I have to get my money back. And the house in Southampton! I can't just go to

L.A. I'm going to suffocate her with lawyers, Rebecca. I'll make sure they squeeze all the air out of her and that she dies of fucking asphyxiation."

"Dad, don't say that."

"I mean it!"

"Maybe I should talk to her."

"I already told you, stay away from her. Just stay away. I mean it!"

He was flipping through the papers on the desk, twitchy, spooked. Rebecca wondered if she shouldn't dial 911. Maybe he needed to be taken away. How did one know? She couldn't leave him here like this, could she?

"I'm begging you, Dad. Let's go to Los Angeles. Please. Please. I can't leave you here. I'm afraid of what will happen."

"Afraid of what?"

"You're not well."

Suddenly, Oliver's left hand seized the back of his head, his eyes widened—some new misery had sprung to mind. Rebecca asked him what.

"The gold. The diamonds. Where are they?"

"What are you talking about?"

"My mother's jewelry. She's taken it all, hasn't she!"

"I don't know what you mean?"

"Oh my God, she has."

The next hour and a half was not unlike an FBI raid. Rebecca watched while her father tore the loft apart. He went room to room. He tried to think like his mother, who would go to great lengths to hide her valuables. So he busted through walls, he used a crowbar on the wood floors beneath his parents' bed, he removed cabinets, cut open the backs of picture frames, emptied out pieces of luggage. He checked the pockets of every coat. He went through his mother's purses. She had dozens.

He used a box cutter on the divan where his father had spent his last months, slicing open the upholstery. He carved into his parents' bed, he looked for loose stones inside coffee canisters and cereal boxes, shook each one, making sure that nothing inside jingled. There were grates everywhere, in the kitchen and the bathroom, in the studio, in the halls—and Oliver un-screwed them all, inspecting behind the metal plates.

While Rebecca was thinking, *Yes, he's lost his mind. I should call an ambulance now. I must. I must.*

Then suddenly her father dropped to the floor. He hadn't fainted, but was seated in a cross-legged position. His eyes were open, he was breathing hard, and his knees were up high. He was sweaty, and seemed drugged—medicated—as if the effort of demolishing the whole loft had worked on him like a horse pill. His head moved side to side. He looked at his daughter.

"She's stolen all of it," he said. "The jewelry, the millions in gold and diamonds—she's stolen every last piece, Rebecca. Don't you see? Look. It's all gone."

VII. OLD LOVE

Over the following days, Rebecca didn't speak with her father. She would later think that she had been in a state of shock. After all, when leaving the loft that night, she had been determined to find her father a doctor. He was in trouble. He needed professional help. She had to get him into a hospital. And then to be in touch his wife. Where was she? It was time Sheila came to New York, confronted her husband, got him out of his parents' bed. Yes, heading home from the loft that night, Rebecca had been intent on pulling in Sheila and any number of doctors who might be able to save her father.

But two weeks on, though she had asked around for a good therapist and had thought about calling her stepmother, Rebecca hadn't followed through on either.

And thank God she hadn't.

This was the opinion of Gertrude Fish, who conveyed her thoughts to her neighbor over a bottle of red wine in her woodshop one night. The carpenter said, to start with, a daughter couldn't rescue her father from self-annihilation, so she shouldn't even go about trying. What a daughter should do with a father whose life was nothing more than a series of mistakes and feuds and crises and poor luck was to let him know that she couldn't do anything for him. That she wasn't made to save him. That that wasn't how the system had been drawn up. That a daughter needed a father to be strong, and that if he couldn't be that in any real way, then he better do his best to fake it. And that if he wasn't any good at acting, then he better take lessons. Or remove himself from the picture. Because a dad without a prayer was a problem for a daughter. So he should put himself somewhere that he couldn't be seen. A place not visible to anyone, and especially not his daughter, since she wasn't put on the earth to watch him suffer. No, a daughter wasn't made for that. Gertrude said that her own father had instilled this wisdom in her by being such a tremendous failure.

"Wasn't he schizophrenic?"

"No, Rebecca. He just didn't know who or what he wanted to be, so every day he was someone different. You're being taken advantage of. The demolition of his parents' home—that was a show, Rebecca. A put on, a stunt, an attempt to make you someone that you're not. That is, his caretaker."

"Gertrude, no. That's not true."

The carpenter vigorously rapped her knuckles on a small can of wood finish, used a flathead screwdriver to pop the lid, and then carefully stirred the dark, thick substance with a paintbrush. As the night wore on, Gertrude would become more and more disheveled. But the time now was 9:30 p.m., and her gray hair was calm on her head, her brown eyes were clear and fresh, her gray jumper unstained. Even the woodshop had an orderliness to it. There were no used sheets of sandpaper on the floor. The jars on the shelf holding every kind of screw and bolt were in their right place. Saws hung by their handles on a long metal spoke that came out of the wall. The floor looked swept. Rebecca was leaning next to an open window, telling Gertrude that her father hadn't thrust his problems on her. If anything, she had invited herself in.

"He would have you think that," Gertrude said. "But don't you see, this is your town now. He can't come back here, set fires in other neighborhoods, and expect you not to smell smoke in your own."

"It's a big city," Rebecca said.

"More like a village," Gertrude replied.

"He has a right to be here."

Gertrude dipped the paintbrush in the can and applied the finish to a small, square piece of wood. She said, "If I were you, Rebecca, I would ask myself, 'Am I my father's daughter? Or, his mother? I mean, don't you want to have children of your own?"

"And the two are related how?"

"Rebecca, you can't be a mother to your own children if you have to be one to your father."

"I won't blame my romantic troubles on him."

"Then tell me about your father's wife. What's she like? Warm? Caring? Maternal?"

"No."

"Of course she isn't. Because if she were any of those things, your father wouldn't be alone here right now, depending on you. He'd be with her, getting what he needs. Now wake up, Rebecca. This is all painfully obvious."

"I am awake."

The next day was a Tuesday in early September. Rebecca was seated in a boardroom on the forty-third floor of a Midtown office building. A meeting about an upcoming IPO offer was supposed to begin in five minutes, but Rebecca was the only person in the large conference room. Her phone began flashing the name "Laura Saks." The device went silent, but only briefly, for now Laura was calling a second time, and then a third. There was a voice message. And after the meeting, while at lunch in an Au Bon Pain, Rebecca acknowledged with a pass of her hand over the back of her neck that she hadn't had any contact with her father for far too long. And where she didn't want to hear Laura's voice—even a recorded version, for she disliked her father's ex-fiancée so intensely—what if she were calling to tell Rebecca that her father was in a hospital, and Rebecca had to get there at once? Or maybe he had done something horrific to himself. Yes, perhaps he had hurt himself.

She pressed for her messages.

"You have one new message. *New message...*'Hi Rebecca, it's Laura. We have to talk. It's about Oliver. He's in trouble. I'm sure you already know. Your aunt really fucked him this time. But don't worry, he's getting out of the loft. I was there yesterday, and I told him that he had to get out and he knows. I have a realtor looking around for him right now, and it should all be settled shortly. We're up against a lot of dangerous people. I promise you, it's going to be okay. I'm taking care of everything. Just call me. I want to make sure you stay informed. Love you. Ciao.'"

Rebecca had another meeting in ten minutes, but she snatched her purse from the back of her chair and hurried outside. On Lexington and Fifty-Second, she hailed a taxi and told the driver the address to the loft. Traffic was slow-moving on the avenue. Rebecca asked if there wasn't a better route.

"It's going to open up on Fortieth Street," the cabbie told her.

"Please," she said. "I'm in a hurry."

But to think how hard she'd had to fight to disentangle herself from Laura Saks.

There's no way I'll let her back in, she said to herself. *No. It won't happen.*

Shortly before Laura and Oliver's third engagement was called off, Oliver began seeing Mandy Sears, a music journalist. At night, Oliver would call Laura and tell her that he was tired, his head hurt, he was out of sorts, he and his sisters had fought all day at the office, he couldn't find a taxi home, and his feet were killing him. Or his back was out of whack, his stomach was in knots, and so he wouldn't be able to see her. That's right, he had to be alone. Why? Because that's just the way it was. He was getting off the phone. Yes, right now. They could talk tomorrow. Would he see her then? Probably not tomorrow. The day after? Perhaps. He was sorry he had been less available these days, he wanted to see her, but no, not tonight.

After getting off the phone with his fiancée, he would take Rebecca aside: he would be having dinner out, he'd be back soon. If Laura called, Rebecca should say that he was asleep. Although she probably wouldn't call because he had just spoken to her and said goodnight. Then he would walk out the door and ride seventy blocks in a taxi to Mandy's apartment on Third Avenue and Tenth Street.

However ugly Rebecca found Mandy Sears—the petite, plump, large-chested blonde would come by the apartment on occasion, but she sought no rapport with her lover's daughter—her father was cheerful in her company. He had no complaints about his health, his day, his life. He laughed, smiled, made jokes, put on good clothes, shaved and combed his hair. To see him try and impress Mandy after an apathetic five years with Laura was encouraging for Rebecca. This remained true for six months. Then Laura learned about the affair.

Rebecca dialed Oliver in the taxi just south of Pete's Tavern. A few people out walking were putting up umbrellas. A white pigeon preened on the bust of Washington Irving outside the high school bearing his name. Her father was on the line now. Rebecca began shouting at once. "What's going on, Dad?"

"Sweetheart, is that you?" There was a clearness to his voice, an energy, which Rebecca hadn't heard for months.

"Laura Saks just left me a terrifically psychotic message. You should probably hear it. It's one for the ages."

Oliver said, "Sweetheart, what happened?"

"What happened, Dad? What happened? You tell me what happened!"

"Well, don't worry about anything."

"What do you mean 'don't worry,' Dad? Tell me what the hell you mean."

"I mean, Laura is helping me with some things."

"Laura Saks?"

"Yes."

"Do you mean it?"

"Yes, I mean it," he answered calmly. "And why not?"

"Well, where to start?" said Rebecca. "How about her head is screwed. And who knows what she's after. It's not worth finding out."

"Rebecca, she wants to find me a new apartment and lend a hand with the lawsuit I'm preparing against Doris."

"Dad, Laura is a goddamn idiot. Please, don't associate with her."

"I understand, Rebecca. I know you're only saying this because you care about me."

"That's right. I am, Dad. Laura can't be trusted. Don't you see that? Whatever she's offering, don't take it."

"Rebecca," her father said, "you have to know that I did everything for her. I let her into my business when we were young. She always copied me and did whatever I did. That's how it was. And her whole life, she's had such confidence issues.

I mean, I was the one she called when she was feeling suicidal. And I was the one who told her she was a talented person, since no one else thought so, and she was so desperate to hear it. What did she do? She stole all the credit for the artists we discovered. I said nothing. *You need the attention*, I thought, *take it.* That was my position. I have more self-respect than that. I know what's valuable in this life, and it has nothing to do with your picture being in a magazine."

"Who are you talking about!" Rebecca cried.

"Doris! Doris!" her father said. Now Oliver began to speak about his mother and their bond and how Eliza would have never written him out of the will, they were too close. He described Ben and Doris pressuring a woman who'd been living with Parkinson's for twenty years and was knocked out by her meds into signing a piece of paper.

"And about Laura," Oliver said, "she's happy to pay for my apartment. I don't have that kind of money. And she has tons. It's okay, sweetheart. I know how to handle her."

Throughout Rebecca's life, her father had told her again and again that he knew how to handle a given person, Ben, for instance, or Laura, Sheila, Doris, or Sondra. The phrase made Rebecca's insides burn. She said, "I'm so worried about you, Dad."

"Don't be. I'm taking care of everything."

Rebecca shook her head. "No," she told her father, "no, this isn't right. It's not. It's just terrible, Dad."

"Sweetheart—"

"Dad, I'm going to open up a bank account for you."

There was silence on the phone. The taxi was stopped on Houston and Wooster, and Rebecca pushed twenty dollars into the driver's hand and slid out of the car. She was saying, "I'm just a minute away. We're going to the bank right now."

"Rebecca—"

"I mean it, Dad. I can afford it."

"Rebecca. I—"

"I'm going to give you the money you need, and you'll promise me that you won't speak to Laura anymore. Just please, promise. Promise, and then put on your shoes and meet me downstairs in five minutes. There's a Citibank on Canal. We'll go right over and set up an account."

"No, Rebecca. I couldn't let you do that."

"Dad, stop it. You will. Now just promise you won't speak to Laura anymore."

Oliver said, "You feel that strongly about it, Rebecca?"

"Yes."

"You do?"

"Yes, Dad!"

A truck was parked outside the loft. Beams for a new scaffold were being shuffled from the truck's bed by construction workers, who stood them upright and assembled them on the sidewalk. Rebecca, only a half block away, could hear their power tools squealing through the phone.

"Well, then that's what we'll do," Oliver said to his daughter. "I'm coming down now."

"Good."

Rebecca leaned against a parking sign. To herself she was saying Laura's name over and over, while recalling the Friday afternoon when Oliver went out of town with Mandy. He hadn't traveled anywhere with her before. How to get away from Laura for a whole day, let alone the entire weekend? His fiancée was always right there, pressing to see him. Before going off, Oliver called Rebecca from his Flatiron District office and told her that if Laura phoned, she should let her know that he wasn't well—a migraine, she was supposed to say—he was asleep and he would call her in the morning.

She said to her father, "No problem. Let Laura know you've got a migraine. You'll talk to her in the morning. Got it."

At 6 p.m., Laura called. Rebecca relayed her father's message.

"Oh?" she said. "Well, if he wakes up, have him phone me. It's important."

"I promise, I will," Rebecca said, and she got off.

An hour passed. Rebecca lay in bed, watching MTV. Then suddenly the phone was ringing again. It was Laura. And was Oliver awake yet? Rebecca said no, he wasn't.

"He must be very sick."

"Yes."

Laura suggested she bring over hot soup. But Rebecca said that that wasn't necessary. In fact, they had split pea in the fridge. And she had been to the pharmacy and bought her father pain relievers and a candy bar. He was fine. Anyhow, she had to go. She hung up the phone.

And yet, a moment later, the old rotary in the kitchen was ringing a third time. The sound, hostile and pestering, daunting, carried through the apartment.

"Hello."

"Rebecca, it's Laura. Wake your father. I have a question to ask him."

"Laura," she began, "he's not well. You want me to wake him?"

"Yes. It's important. Tell him it'll just take a second."

"I don't think I should."

"Well, you have to, Rebecca."

Rebecca stuttered over the phone's large black mouthpiece. "Laura, I don't know."

"Go and get your father."

"He'll be angry."

"Do it. Tell him it's an emergency."

Rebecca set the phone on the kitchen counter and walked into the apartment where Laura had come to live the year before, only to leave one day three months later, and toward Oliver's bedroom. She called out, "Dad! Hey, Dad, it's Laura! She wants to talk to you." She let the Mississippis run off. *One Mississippi. Two Mississippi. Three Mississippi. Four Mississippi.*

"Nope," she told Laura, having returned to the phone. "He won't wake up."

"What do you mean, 'won't wake up?' Did you tell him it's an emergency?"

"Yes. And he said he'll call you in the morning."

"So you said it was an emergency, and he said he would call me in the morning?"

It had sounded strange to her too, but she said, "Right."

"You're serious?"

"What can I tell you, Laura? What do you want me to do?"

"You told him it's an emergency, and he still wouldn't get on the phone? That's what you're telling me?"

"Yes, Laura."

"Lies."

"What?"

"Is your father even there?"

"He is."

"Then put him on the phone, *now.*"

"I'm not waking him again."

"Do it, Rebecca!"

"No!"

Laura hung up.

Not ten minutes later, the lock was turning in the front door. A wave of terror passed through Rebecca, and she rushed from her bedroom. There, in the doorway, she saw Laura's short, stooped figure. Her brown eyes stared out chaotically from a panting, red face. Pointing at Rebecca with her set of keys to the apartment, she said, "He's not here, is he?"

"I'm sorry, Laura."

Then Laura said, "Fuck him," and left.

Rebecca called her father at the hotel upstate, and told him what had happened. She was crying. She said, "I tried, Dad. But it was like she knew everything from the start."

Oliver told her not to worry, that this wasn't her problem, he would handle it.

Having been caught cheating, Rebecca thought that her father's relationship with Laura was over. But Laura continued to show up at the apartment. She would eat dinner with Rebecca and her father and spend the night perhaps three times a week. The strain was there in her face, though. The grim, souring effects of disembowelment. The misery. What had Oliver told her to keep her around? That she'd misjudged the situation? That he'd been meeting with a recording artist, locally, for the purposes of business and nothing more? Whatever his story, Rebecca could see the life force had slipped from Laura. Oliver wasn't putting in any extra effort to please her, either. In fact, after two weeks, he started to push against her, same as always. He couldn't see her, his legs were tired, a nerve in his back was pinched. Nevertheless, they were still engaged. Laura's toothbrush remained in the glass on the sink. A few times a week Rebecca heard Laura's key turning in the lock at the front door. She wasn't gone just yet.

And then she was.

Oliver told his daughter about it one day. They were in the mailroom, a narrow hall of mirrors and small, shimmering metal doors in the lobby of the building. He said, "Laura won't be coming around anymore."

"Thank God," Rebecca said. "I couldn't bear another day of her."

"Me neither," her father laughed.

Months passed without any sign of Laura. No one had spoken to her, or seen her on the street, or heard anything of her whereabouts.

But then one day, Laura called the apartment. Rebecca answered. And Laura was all of a sudden rambling about how they had to make a date to meet. It was very important, they would have dinner, Laura already knew where. Should it be tomorrow night or over the weekend? Rebecca said she had no free time right now. But a week later, Laura called again. She left a message. She had to see Rebecca, it was urgent, she couldn't wait another day. The fifteen-year-old girl didn't tell her father. She didn't want to bother him. He was with Mandy Sears, and, for the first time in years, he seemed happy. Besides, Rebecca could deal with Laura herself.

However, Laura was so persistent. She kept pushing. "Let's do dinner." "I have to see you." "Please."

Eventually, Rebecca gave in.

She went to meet Laura one night at her apartment on Columbus and Seventy-Sixth. Before she could get inside the door, the sulking, beat-upon woman was telling Rebecca about all the therapy she'd needed after the split with her father. She said her life had fallen apart, and she'd been slowly putting it back together. The teenager noted the toll of Laura's grief. New lines scored her forehead. Her eyes revealed an especially fragile inner self. They ate at an Italian restaurant on Columbus. Laura said she was friends with the owner. They sat at a table in the corner, surrounded by stock photos of the Tuscan landscape. The ex-fiancée asked Rebecca how her father was doing. Before Rebecca could answer, however, Laura interrupted her to say how sorry she was that things hadn't worked out with "Dad."

"The thing is, Oliver has problems. I mean, I have problems. We all do, Rebecca. That's just it—life is full of problems. But some of us, some of us have far more problems than others. And when I say far more, I mean to say that there are some seriously fucked-up people out there. Okay, Rebecca? You understand?"

"I do."

"And these are just facts."

"Hmm-mmm." Rebecca's brown eyes rose with her breath. Clearly the evening would be a very long one.

The waiter appeared, a young, energetic man with a thin black mustache. Laura asked Rebecca if she wanted any wine. "No," she said.

Laura insisted.

"That's okay," Rebecca told the waiter.

Laura, seeming to take Rebecca's refusal personally, said, "Not even a little?"

"Thank you. No."

"Fine. Screw Driver, Stoli, for me," said Laura. The ex-fiancée hovered over the table with elbows set wide. Pale and anxious, impatient, she said, "What you have to understand is that I tried to save your father. I *tried*, Rebecca. I wanted to get him past the feelings he had for your mother. There was nothing I could do. He couldn't let go of them. I'm not sure if he will ever fully recover from his divorce. I mean, who knows."

"Yes."

"And his family is so fucked. His sisters, his parents—they'll try to kill him. They don't care, they'll take everything they can from him. But you know that."

"I do."

"I offered your dad a way out, Rebecca. A hundred times I said, 'Come with me. Forget these people.' He wouldn't do it." Laura's head moved side to side in small, manic circles. She said, "Could you imagine being the child of Ben Arkin? And Eliza isn't any better. You see, I know things. I was right there, and saw it all."

"Sure, Laura. I know you did."

The ex-fiancée, her cheeks becoming a darker red hue, her arms lifting out to the sides, said, "But he needs you. Your father needs you. You know that, don't you?"

"I do, Laura."

"Do you?"

"Yes," said the girl. "But it's all right now. Dad's well. You don't have to worry about him."

But it was apparent from the ex-fiancée's look that she didn't believe this. Taking a menu in her hands, Laura noted that the specials were always delicious. "Did I tell you my friend owns this place?"

"Yes. You did."

And yet the worst repetitions were still to come. The bread and water not even on the table, Laura began saying:

"Rebecca, see, what you have to understand is that I did everything I could for your father. I wanted it to work out. I did. You know that, right? I did everything I could. I tried."

"I know, Laura."

Over the white tablecloth, the ex-fiancée stared solemnly at Rebecca. "But you grew up in that apartment. It was a sad place, Rebecca. Your father was so troubled—because of your mother. Oliver loved her long after the divorce. He was devastated after she left him. You don't know the things I know. Because I'm older. All right. I was divorced, too. Did you know that?"

Laura had told her many times. But Rebecca said, "You've never mentioned it, no."

"Oh, well, yeah, I was married. I was young. What can I say—very young and stupid. He was a decent man, it just didn't work out. Soon after my divorce I met your father. It wasn't an easy time for me. Divorce is very, very emotional. Very difficult. But the thing about your father—what I truly think…"

"Yes?"

"He was afraid, Rebecca. Your father was…afraid to get hurt again, to feel again, to put himself in a place where he could experience love."

Rebecca told her she agreed. What else could she do? Run?

In fact, running came later. First, there was the next decade, in which Rebecca and Laura continued to meet every few months. Their list of restaurants expanded, but their topics of conversation remained at one: Oliver. Laura could speak of nothing else. Even a whole nine years later, her diction was the same.

"The thing is, I tried. I did."

"I know you did."

"It was that he wasn't ready to love again. Divorce can be very painful."

"Sure. Yes. I understand that."

Laura's recapitulations confused, even frightened, Rebecca. Did Laura know she was repeating herself? This was what old people did. Laura was only in her mid-fifties then. But her relationship with Oliver had aged her prematurely. Or perhaps just rotted her head. Either way, these dinners exhausted Rebecca. And did they have to meet again? No. No, Rebecca wouldn't do it.

But then, a month later, Laura would telephone Rebecca. And after another cycle of messages and unreturned calls, Rebecca's conscience would buckle, and she would dial Laura.

On one occasion, Laura said it was good that she had—she wanted to take Rebecca to Barney's. Yes. And she could buy anything she wanted. So she should be there tomorrow at noon.

The following day, they met outside the department store, on Madison Avenue. Right away, Rebecca began to apologize to Laura for having taken so long to be in touch. Laura, with a white sun hat, cream-colored linen suit, and a red leather clutch under her arm, was telling the young woman how there was no need to apologize, that she understood, because they went back so many years.

"It's true, you've known me since I was a little girl," Rebecca said. "But I'm not a little girl anymore. You realize that, don't you?"

Laura said, "Well, yes. Sure I do."

"You do?"

"Yes."

"Good, Laura. Then I want you to listen to me. I don't want to talk about my father anymore. All right? I can't do it. From now on, let's stop all that. Please."

"Oh. Oh yeah. Yeah, that's fine," Laura said, flashing a knee-weakened look.

"It's not helpful for me, or us, or you."

"Yes. Yes, I know."

"Let's talk about anything else."

Laura raised a hand in the air, pausing. Half her face trembled and her small brown eyes looked upward to the sky. One tear fell, and then another. She said, "I've spent ten years in therapy speaking about your father. And you know what, I've also had enough of it. You'll never hear me mention him again."

"Laura, you don't have to—"

"No! No, I'm sorry. You're right. I'll never talk about your father again."

Her position was extreme. But let her begin with extremes, thought Rebecca, then work her way back to some better place.

After shopping, they dined at the same Italian restaurant owned by Laura's friend. It turned out, when not hearing about her parents' divorce, her father's hang-ups, or how Laura had really tried to make the relationship with Oliver work, Rebecca found the food actually very good. There was still plenty to discuss. Laura's plans to build a home upstate, for instance. Well, it hadn't been so interesting to Rebecca. But she was grateful that Laura had changed subjects. An hour later, after espresso and tiramisu, Laura explained that she could use Rebecca's assistance with her new iMac. She didn't understand computers. It was something she attributed to helping a college boyfriend dodge the Vietnam War. The truth, Rebecca decided, was unimportant. She said she would be happy to show her father's ex-fiancée how to use the computer.

She returned to Laura's home a week later. An open house was underway in the apartment across the hall. Laura told Rebecca that the owners were asking four million.

"Can you believe that?"

"I guess you don't have to worry about money," Rebecca said.

"Well, no, everyone has to worry about money, Rebecca, particularly those who have it. Take your father. He has money, but he was raised rich, and wants as much of it as he can get. I wish I'd had more. I gave him as much as I could."

"I know," Rebecca said.

"I didn't have any more to spare."

"I understand," said Rebecca, offering a simple, cool nod.

They went to Zabar's. At the fish counter, admiring the smoked salmon and sturgeon in the display case, Laura said she would like to eat everything in the store but that she was trying to stay lean.

"I've come to realize that if you don't take care of yourself, no man will look at you. So I work hard to keep myself in shape. It leaves a person feeling more mentally fit, too. After your father left me, it was like I gave up, you know? I ate so much junk and put on all this weight. It was very hard to care." With her chin lowered, using all her power to show she was in control now, she said, "But your father, you know—"

"Yes—"

"He did a number on me. I went away afterward. One month at a rehab facility."

"I know. And I'm sorry."

"Oh, I wasn't going to make it on my own. I needed help. That was a tough thing I went through. You remember. You were there."

"I was."

"That night."

"Yes—what a night. And I am sorry about it."

"It left me very…damaged."

Rebecca had no doubt about that. "I wish it hadn't happened," she said.

"That woman your father ran off with…Mindy. No, Mandy. It hurt me. It still does."

"I'm sure," said Rebecca. However, she wouldn't be taken advantage of for another second. She spoke up. She said, "Laura, I came today thinking we wouldn't discuss my father. Let's not do it."

Laura's head moved up and down. "I know. I'm sorry. You're right, we don't need to talk about it. We don't need to."

The fish slicer called their number, and Laura encouraged Rebecca to order a few of pounds of everything.

"You like sable?"

"No," Rebecca said. "Thank you."

"Oh, don't be shy. She'll take a pound of nova, a pound of whitefish, a pound of sturgeon, a pound of kippered salmon…"

On Broadway, Rebecca, her hands overwhelmed by shopping bags, said goodbye. Before she could get away, though, Laura promised that she would do better next time. She wouldn't talk about Oliver even once. It wouldn't be difficult. She'd only needed a little practice. And now that she'd had it, consider her ready to go. Rebecca said she looked forward to it. She wouldn't tell Laura that their days of shopping and dining were over.

But one day, four months later, Rebecca was reading in Washington Square Park. By then she was enrolled at NYU Law School. Beautiful late spring weather, and thousands of students out with the sun. Rebecca was sitting on a bench not far from the arch, having a coffee. Suddenly, Laura was standing right in front of her. The appearance of his father's ex-fiancée greatly startled Rebecca, who gathered her things and stood.

"Laura! How are you?"

Laura looked much older now. This was in large part due to her hair being cut to within an inch of her scalp. "Rebecca, hello. Surprised to see you here. Yeah, I'm doing well."

"That's great," said Rebecca.

"You know, I've called you ten times. You don't call me back."

Rebecca, zipping up her bag, beginning to walk, hid nothing. She said, "I told you I didn't want to talk about my father. But you couldn't help yourself."

"I know it upsets you, Rebecca. I know."

"Well, we can't meet again."

"We can't?"

"No, I don't want to see you."

"You mean that?" Laura said.

Rebecca considered how many times her father had broken things off with Laura. Now she was doing the same. She felt bad for the woman. But she wouldn't back down. She said, "I mean it, yes. We won't be seeing each other anymore."

"So that's how it has to be?"

"Yes."

"You're serious?"

"I am, yes."

Laura released a short, violent grunt. "Well, I guess I'll see you around then."

"No, you won't, Laura."

"You know what," the woman shouted, "you're just as bad as any of them!"

"Please. Just stay away from me!"

"So long!" Laura screamed.

Rebecca didn't believe this was the end of Laura. Why should she? Her father's ex-fiancée, desperate for any sort of contact with Oliver, would find a way of talking herself back to the phone, and dialing Rebecca. And yet, over the eight years that followed, Rebecca heard nothing from Laura. On several occasions, and for no apparent reason, Rebecca would think of Laura and a private celebration would break out within her. It had been such hard work getting rid of her.

And now?

Rebecca heard a door close—Oliver was stepping out onto the sidewalk. She saw that her father had put on his checkered suit and combed his gray hair straight back. He looked exhausted. But he had spent the past three weeks in that dark room, and here he was outside, in the sun, and this in itself was an achievement. He unfolded a pair of black sunglasses, slipped them over his eyes, brought his fingers through his hair, and said, "Shall we?"

Rebecca said, "Let's." But at once she wondered, *How much will I give him a month? Four thousand to start. That's going to make things tight. No more spending on anything but the very essentials. No matter, I'm happy to do this. What a thing to be able to do. He supported me the first twenty-five years of my life. That's a long time. I owe him this. Just happy to do it. Anything to make things easier on him. Look how calm he seems.*

She threw her arm around her father's waist and pulled him tightly to her side. "I'm glad to see you out. It's a big step."

He kissed her on the head. "Thank you," he said.

They turned onto bustling Canal Street. Rebecca could feel her father's body slightly lift, the Citibank now in view. To herself, she was saying, *But why shouldn't he be excited? It's nice to be supported, if you can find someone to do it. You'll give him whatever he needs, Rebecca. He's your father.*

Yet now she was saying, "Dad, before we go on...," and she took Oliver by the arm. "You have to promise me you won't speak to Laura."

With the sunglasses slid halfway down his nose, Oliver said, "I can't stand her."

By answering in this indirect way, Rebecca didn't know if she had to ask again for him to promise. However, they couldn't remain here. The sidewalk was thronged with tourists buying knock-off leather bags from black-market vendors. She said to her father, "I don't want you to let her get involved in any lawsuits."

"No—"

"Or for you to have anything to do with her."

"I won't."

"This is the start of intelligent decisions."

"Rebecca, I have to do what's best for me. There's still a lot I mean to do. I have to get a new record label going, make my own money, support myself. I can't let people like Laura take up my energy."

"She's not well."

"And I have to be smart." He was becoming somewhat impassioned now, using his whole body to speak. "This is my life we're talking about. I can't let anything get in the way of my health or my business."

"Right," said Rebecca, still waiting to be satisfied. "You'll have to start working very soon."

"I plan on it. I have to earn money."

"You do. That's right, Dad. Because I can't afford to support you for too long and keep my apartment. My mortgage is a lot, you know?"

"I understand," he said.

"But for now," she told him, "let's set up your account. Come on."

"Okay, honey. Just one more thing."

"What's that?"

"I'd like it…" he said. "I'd like it if we didn't tell my wife about this."

Rebecca had been holding open the door to the bank, but now she let go and asked her father, "Why?"

"It's just that Sheila wants to make all my decisions for me—and I'm done with it. She doesn't even live here, you know? And it's just, it's my life. And I don't need her, or anyone, telling me what to do. I know what's best for me. So that's just it, Rebecca. You know what I mean?"

She had no idea what he meant. But she said to him, "I suppose I do, Dad. But after you move out of the loft, won't Sheila want to know who's paying the rent for your new apartment?"

"She already thinks Laura will be paying for it."

"And she's all right with Laura paying?"

"She is."

"How can that be?"

"Because," Oliver said, "Sheila has no money to give me. And I have no money of my own. So she has no choice but to be all right with it. You understand?"

"No. I can't say I do," Rebecca said.

"Well, don't get yourself upset over it."

"But will you still tell Sheila that Laura's paying your rent?"

Bending deeply at the knees, Oliver sighed. "That's what I was planning on doing. Unless you have a better idea."

Rebecca thought for a moment. However, nothing came to mind, and she shook her head and told her father, "It's not constructive to lie to your wife about this."

"I agree," he said. "I totally agree."

"It's just that all of a sudden Sheila might think you can ask Laura for more and more money, and I want to eliminate the very idea of that from the start."

"You're right. You're absolutely right." Oliver looked far down Canal Street at cars lining up at the entrance to the Holland Tunnel. Slightly withdrawn, he said, "We'll tell her it's a watch, then."

"Dad." She glowered at her father. "Don't just humor me. I'm being serious."

Oliver said, "I'm not just humoring you. We'll tell her it's a...a couple of watches. My grandfather's watches."

What Rebecca wanted now was for this conversation to end. She said, "It's getting late. The bank's closing soon. Let's just go inside and start filling out the paperwork."

"Great," he said. "I'm ready for that, sweetie."

VIII: MOTHER HELP ME

At 11 a.m. on a Friday morning, Rebecca was on her way to her father's new apartment across the street from the Morgan Library. At her father's door, she rang the bell. He didn't answer. She tried again, and then took out a spare key and went inside. As she had hoped, he wasn't there. She locked the door behind her. Next thing, she switched on the lights. She looked in the fridge and found it empty, only a water pitcher with many thin discs of lemon floating at the top and a half-eaten chocolate bar occupying the butter compartment on the door. She peeked into her father's closets, sifted through his drawers, examined the contents of the medicine cabinet in the bathroom. She saw the laundry basket, and checked the pockets of his dirty pants. She lifted up the cushions of the sofa, she dug her fingers under the mattress in the bedroom. There was a suitcase beside the dresser. Nothing was inside. Oliver used to hide money in record sleeves. Was there the time to look through his vast LP collection? Who knew when he would return? She should leave. She checked to make sure that she had left everything as she'd found it. Then she noticed that his living room windows looked directly at the McKim Building. One of the architectural gems of the city—a strong, Neoclassical marble container made to house and protect one of the great collections of books. From its arched entrance, flanked by lions, an elegant glass lamp hung between two soft white columns, and behind it were two steel doors. That her father was able to see this building from his window was very fortunate for him, thought Rebecca.

She went into a deli around the corner. At an ATM toward the back, she pressed for a balance on her father's account. Oliver had called her last week to describe feelings of gratitude and relief. He'd told her how, in the mornings, he had been shooting out of bed, rested, hungry for food, for art and conversation, that all his grand ambitions about his career had been inching closer to reality, that he had been employing a new physical regimen involving a strict diet, regular exercise, and a consistent sleep schedule that would leave him in better shape than ever before.

Rebecca hadn't believed a word of it.

Among shelves of pet food products, cleaning powders, garbage bags, and votary candles, she took the ATM receipt, reading $7,802.10, in her left hand. The opening balance had been fifteen thousand. She'd put in three thousand more just five days ago. How had her father spent over ten grand in such a short time? Other than the bed frame and the mattress, had he made any large purchases? There'd been the incident two weeks earlier with the toaster. Four hundred dollars. She'd forced him to return it and take a more simple model. Then they'd had to have the talk: she didn't want to have to look over his shoulder, but he had to act more responsibly. Because she was supporting him now, she bought only the very essentials and he had to do the same. Did he understand what she meant by "the very essentials"? Food, transportation, rent, utilities, and some forms of entertainment. Movies, yes. Operas, no. A record was fine, but no box sets. Her father had answered by wrapping his hands around her shoulders and kissing her on the head.

At the moment, she was wondering about his rent, though. Twenty-five hundred a month, he had told her. Perhaps there was first and last month's plus security deposit to factor in. Yes, maybe that explained it.

Rebecca started uptown on a bright but withdrawn stretch of Madison Avenue, criticizing herself for having searched her father's apartment. How was he supposed to find respect for himself if his own daughter couldn't show him any? She spoke an apology out loud, to no one, and then closed her lips over the knuckles of her right hand—a half block north, leaning against the Joseph Raphael De Lamar House, the Beaux-Arts mansion, reading the *New York Times*, was Oliver. His gray, slicked-back hair had grown a little long and he had a wispy white beard. At all the people passing, he smiled with a wrinkled, pleasant look. In the way he folded the newspaper, his eyes making a periodic sweep of the pedestrians, Rebecca sensed a sort of fraudulent majesty about him. He wore his checkered suit with a red kerchief folded neatly in the pocket. And with this outfit, he was trying to fool himself into thinking he'd gotten up this morning with a purpose? He had to get a job. But what kind? He was too old to go back into the record business. He didn't have the energy or the money for it. He could work for someone else. But who would hire him? No sensible executive would invest time and resources in a man over sixty. And yet, he had to do something with his life.

Rebecca followed him west, toward Fifth Avenue. He entered a bistro at the middle of the block, ordered at the bar, and began talking with the waitstaff. A young woman with dark hair and olive skin and a nice smile indulged him. But what could they be discussing? Was he not boring her? Did she not speak to him out of pity?

Rebecca watched from behind a parked pickup truck, her dark, tremulous eyes narrowed and her tongue bent back against her top teeth. But to tell your daughter you were waking up early every day to figure out your life and then to sleep till noon instead. To have hardly a dime to your name and still spend the midday hours reading the paper and lunching and socializing with waitresses. To give up and feel comfortable with it. While being supported by your child.

Rebecca asked herself how long she could let this go on.

Sitting down on the rear bumper of the pickup truck, she dialed her father's wife. It was time they spoke. On the side street, shaded from the sun by tall buildings, Rebecca heard the phone click.

"I was just about to call you," Sheila said, as a greeting.

"Oh, were you?"

"Yes. I wanted you to know Doris is being served with papers today."

Placing her hand across her neck, her skin sending heat back through her fingers, Rebecca said, "Well, this seems a bit hurried, don't you think? Does my father even have a case?"

"Yes."

"A winnable case?"

"The attorneys say the odds are at least seventy-thirty in our favor, and that we're not even going to get into a courtroom. We're looking for a quick settlement. Everyone has a life to get back to. We don't want to be doing this forever."

"Then you should know that these things take forever, Sheila."

"Yes. I was thinking it would go faster if you helped us."

"I don't know estate law."

"Talk to our lawyers. They might have ways of making use of you."

"Sheila, what I was thinking was that my dad would go back to Los Angeles and take a respite from New York. Some distance will be healing for him."

"I'm in the process of closing the last store, Rebecca. I had to sell my home to pay off my debts."

"Okay, but—"

"There's no room in the motel where I am. And with the two dogs."

"So you've got space for your dogs, but not your husband?"

"Hey, listen! I love your father, but I didn't sign up for all this shit, okay? I mean, can you imagine marrying a man, and the next thing you know, having done nothing at all, his sister's suing you because she's whacked and has nothing better to do? And suddenly you're embroiled in a lawsuit, paying for lawyers, because you must, or else? And now with Doris stealing your father's inheritance."

Rebecca apologized. Defending herself against Sondra had cost Sheila a lot of money. Her aunt's legal complaint? That Sheila had put *Shout!* records on sale at her boutiques. Just three or four, near the register. Not one copy had even sold. But Sondra had sent a spy. The records had been seen, and Sondra had accused Sheila of stealing *Shout!* inventory.

Originally Sheila hadn't even thought that she would marry Oliver, already fifty-seven by the time they'd met and having lived without a husband all her life, along the beach, with her dogs, never lonely. Besides, during the first two years with Oliver, a long-distance relationship had worked well for her. Together one month out of every three, and the rest of the time speaking by phone—no, she had never required more of him. But after her heart attack, Oliver had come to California and taken care of her, and she had asked him to stay.

"I didn't know that I had married into a whole family of psychotics."

"You've faced a lot these last three years," Rebecca said.

"You bet your ass I have."

"But we have to put distance between my father and all of this grief. It's been strictly funerals and strife since he returned to New York. Can't you rent an apartment or get a larger motel room and just let him stay with you for a couple of weeks?"

"With what money, Rebecca? I'm broke. Those boutiques killed me."

"I'm sorry."

"I spend my days on eBay, auctioning off everything just to pay the debt."

Rebecca swept her thumb beneath her front teeth, deciding to change subjects. "The lawyers you're considering, how are you going to pay them?"

"I don't know," Sheila said. "We'll figure out a way. But that sociopath Doris wants to ruin your dad's life, and we can't let her get away with it."

"But you don't even know how you'll pay for this."

"I'm working on it, Rebecca, every second of every day. You understand that the whole thing is very sad to us, don't you? Your aunt, Sondra, suing your grandfather…your grandfather had a huge debt to his lawyers. A million, easy. Those fucking devils."

"Right. Yes. I do."

"Your grandfather bullied your dad, tricked him into giving him most of the money he'd made when he sold his apartment. It was all your father had left. And your grandfather told your father that he would get the money back."

"My father's said as much."

"But that wasn't what happened."

"No. It wasn't."

"Your dad has been fucked too hard to stand by and do nothing."

"I know."

"So then you see why we have to do this. Now really, if you want to help your father, what you should do is go to him, talk to him, take him to dinner, make sure he's getting out. Your dad loves you. You're his only family. There's no one else now."

Rebecca said, "Okay, Sheila."

"Be a good daughter."

"Right. Thanks. I will."

Rebecca got off the phone. Then she watched her father eat a bouillabaisse. After which a digestif and an espresso were set down before him on the counter, and he drank them both. Next he retired to the bathroom for nearly fifteen minutes. He left the bistro with a glowing sweaty presentiment, his pants pulled up higher than when he had entered, and went home—to nap, presumably—while Rebecca returned to her office.

September 21st, 2015

Dear Mom,

I know you're busy. When the film is done, though, I'd like to come visit. It's a strange time. My dad is broke and I've been supporting him to the tune of half my salary. He also happens to be suing his sister Doris over their parents' estate. I'm not sure what to do about any of it. But I'd like to tell you all these things in person, if it works with your schedule. Let me know.

Love, Rebecca

October 1st, 2015

Dear Rebecca,

Darling, I'm sorry to hear about your father. You know my sister Ella has caused me more problems than I care to discuss. I thought all those years ago when I moved to the West Coast that she would stop showing up at my door with her bags. Wrong. She did it three months ago, for the second time this year. I turned her away, and I suggest you do the same with your father. Now if you like, you're welcome to come stay with me in Los Angeles. But it doesn't mean I'd be available all that time, and I don't want to disappoint you. Let's figure something out.

Love you, Mom

October 18th, 2015

Dear Mom,

Don't be so hard on your sister, please. I know she's a strain. But I'm telling you firsthand, it could be much worse. She's never sued you. She's never stolen from you. She isn't a bad person. Treat her right. I'll watch from a distance and be encouraged by it.

Love, Rebecca

November 7th, 2015

Dear Rebecca,

I apologize it's taken me this long to get back to you. My shooting schedule has made it impossible. Don't ever compare yourself with my sister. You're nothing like Ella. You are a highly intelligent, extremely competent, successful person who has worked hard to get where you are. Ella is an emotional tyrant who takes advantage of people who don't have the stamina to combat her. You are a hundred times the person she is. So don't compare yourself to her. You're dissatisfied with your place? That's nearly every person. Now here's some tough love: do something about it. Throw yourself into new territory. Get to it. I love you. I believe in you.

Your Mom

November 18th, 2015

Dear Mom,

I didn't compare myself to your sister. I said that you should treat your sister better. Slow down and read what I write, please.

Love, Rebecca.

P.S. I like my life.

November 30th, 2015

Dear Rebecca,

I am sorry, honey. I didn't mean to upset you. Are you all right? If you want to come and stay with me, you should just do it. Get away from New York and this situation with your father. I can't promise that I'll be available. But you'll have the whole house to yourself. You can swim in the pool and the beach isn't far. If you want, I'll rent you a car and you can take a trip up the coast. There are beautiful places to see. The offer stands. You don't have to decide right now. I might even have time around the New Year, so that I could spend part of that trip with you. Tell me, sweetheart, how much money are you giving your father? I remember how important it was to you that you saved for an apartment. Don't compromise your future, not for anyone. You have to take care of yourself and your needs. I know it sounds cruel and selfish. I just don't want you to jeopardize the things that are important to you. I certainly don't want you to hurt your life in any way.

Love, Mom

December 8th, 2015

Dear Mom,

There's a conversation I had last year with my grandfather Ben that I'd like to tell you about. We were in his studio and he was in a bad way, talking to me about how much he owed the attorneys who defended him in the lawsuit against Sondra. He kept saying, "I'm a poor man, Rebecca. A poor, poor man." Can you imagine a person who had firsthand experience of Depression Era poverty, sitting in his multi-million-dollar SoHo loft with his multimillion-dollar house in the Hamptons just a short car ride away, going on about how he was poor? What does that mean, Mom? It confuses and frightens me. There's some fundamental principle to money which I don't understand. But I should figure it out before I spend my whole life worrying about the stuff. You, too, maybe?

Love, Rebecca

December 28th, 2015

Dear Rebecca,

Seems you're feeling a bit philosophical these days, so I'm going to give it to you straight: Shut the door on your father, right now. It's the only way to deal with his kind. He will take as much as you let him. You have to say, "Enough," and then erect a barricade. It's not selfishness. No, it's called being practical. You're a single woman. The world doesn't treat you with the tenderness you would like it to, so stop treating it as if it did. Toughen up. Get mean. Your survival depends on it. It took me a long time to learn this, but I did. I'm not going to tell you that the result is perfect. I struggle with life. I am unhappy a lot of the time. But I live under my terms. No one can pull me a hundred yards this way and hundred yards that. There's stability in knowing this. Unfortunately, *part of making the decision to not let people walk all over you and take take take is that you will have to feel bad at times. Bad for saying no. Bad for shutting out. Bad for the things they might do to themselves after you have acted. This makes it an imperfect solution. But it does work most of the time, and those are the kinds of answers you have to start believing in. Things that work most of the time, or more often than they do not work, are where you can find improvement. I don't talk to my sister anymore. I haven't for six months anyway. It feels great. I am in control. Me, not her. If Ella showed up at my door, and I suspect she might one of these days, I wouldn't let her in. I'd feel terrible about that for a couple of days. Far better than letting her inside and giving her the privilege of degrading me with her emotions and her needs. That is a month-long recovery. Two months. No, no, no, my dear, save yourself. Don't be railroaded by the same people anymore. Don't be their little whipping girl.*

Love, Your Mom

"…Of course, your sister is emotionally erratic. She's exhausting. She doesn't socialize well."

"But she faults me for hiding her from friends and colleagues."

"Did she forget the last time we took her with us to a party? She cornered Diane's husband in a bathroom."

"She's always been very easy."

"She has no self-confidence."

"And still I feel so bottled up around her. I can't say what's on my mind. Ella's emotions, her sensitivities, have to be attended to. You have to protect her and yourself by not saying the wrong thing. What about my emotions? Ella would say that I don't have any. That nothing seems to bother me. I always seem so together. While she's rigged the world to take pity on her."

"She's clever that way. At any given time, a dozen people are carrying out some favor for Ella. They give her money, a place to stay. They think she's an artist deserving handouts."

"But she's not, Oliver. She might have been. Her photos showed so much potential. It's frustrating to talk about. See, I get worked up. My face overheats, my hands shake, because I believed in her, and what did she do with her talent? Her life? Nothing. She's thirty-eight and still waiting for it to begin."

Helen went to stand before the windows. A blizzard was overtaking the city. The weather report said a foot of snow by morning.

"This is my home. I should never feel uncomfortable here. Not for any reason."

"Don't worry, Helen, she'll leave soon."

"But I'm concerned about Rebecca, too."

"Why me?" asked Rebecca. The eight-year-old had been on the sofa with her head in her father's lap, listening to her parents.

"I don't like you being around her so much. Who knows what kinds of things she tells you. Likely badmouthing me all afternoon while I'm out. 'Your mother's a hard-hearted bitch. She doesn't care that I have no money and no place to go, she wants me gone.'"

"She doesn't do that," Rebecca assured her mother.

"Rebecca's happy to have her here," Oliver said. "You get along well with each other, don't you? I know you find the time after school lonesome."

Rebecca didn't answer. She was watching her mother at the window, in her white bathrobe with the belt untied, her dark chin-length hair gathered in both her hands, her legs strong and shoulders back and her head bent forward.

All of a sudden, Helen said, "Did you put the car in a lot, Oliver?"

"What's that?"

"I said, did you put the car in a lot?"

"No."

"You should have."

"Well, I didn't."

"You should do it now."

"Now?"

"Yes, now."

Oliver said, "Don't be crazy."

"We spend a fortune on that car."

"I know we do."

"But you'd just leave it outside in a snowstorm?"

"Yes."

"It has to go in a lot."

"I'll take care of it in the morning," he said. "I'll dig it out if I have to."

"I'm not leaving the car in the snow, Oliver."

"Helen."

"It's just terrible for the body."

"I'm not worried about the body."

"Well, I am. And I'm moving it."

"Helen!"

But now Helen went to dress. Oliver brought his daughter up to sit. Glaring at her, he said, "Well, we can't let her go alone, can we!"

Oliver remembered parking the BMW the previous afternoon three blocks from the apartment, on Eighty-Third. But outside, every step was a challenge and he didn't want to be wrong. He began to doubt himself. Was it Eighty-Third? First he led his wife and daughter down Eighty-Second. But when he didn't see the car, he said to them, "It's not this block. Come, let's go! Let's go!" and he pulled his daughter by the hand to the next street. He didn't notice his black scarf dragging through the snow, then coming off altogether. When he got to the car, he touched his neck where the scarf had been. Then he looked back down the empty street.

"Damn!" he cried.

"Did you lose your scarf, Dad?"

He didn't reply.

Helen and Rebecca got inside the black car while Oliver scraped snow from the windshield with his forearm. The engine warmed. Not many people were driving, though there weresome taxis in the street. The sanitation trucks did the plowing. Along the curb, garbage bags that wouldn't be picked up for days were halfway disappeared under the snow. The windows were still defogging when Oliver got in the car. He began hitting switches, trying to bring up the temperature inside, muttering angry words under his breath. Removing a glove, Helen licked the end of her middle finger and took a speck of dust off the dashboard.

"Ms. Wyse called today," she said to her husband.

"Who?"

"My assistant principal," said Rebecca, from the back seat.

"She informed me that Ella's been late to pick Rebecca up every day this week, even after I told her that she had to be on time and she promised me she could be depended on."

"Is that true, Rebecca?"

"Yes," she said. "But—"

"Did you speak with Ella?" Oliver asked his wife.

"I did, this evening."

"And…"

"And, no, she wasn't apologetic."

"Why haven't you said anything about it, Rebecca?" The radio whispered news in the background. Oliver shut it off with a violent tap of his forefinger to the black knob.

"Because she's very protective of my sister," Helen interjected. She had been waiting days to say this to her husband, and her daughter. "What, you disagree, Rebecca?"

Rebecca brought her hands together in her lap, saying nothing. Oliver grimaced, the snow obscuring his visibility. The black car drifted down Park Avenue and he felt as if not he but someone else was in control of it.

"From the way Rebecca looks at me since my sister arrived, I know she blames me for the way her life is. You think I should fix everything for Ella, as if I haven't already tried."

"I don't think that, Mom."

But with her head turned toward the window, Helen said, "I won't do it anymore," repeating the phrase again and again. She didn't pause when the car skidded out. She seemed not to notice how Oliver grappled with the steering. Had she not seen the other vehicles stuck in the snow? The only people on the street were those out of their cars helping to push. Rebecca watched their tires spinning, the exhaust pumping out under the diffuse orange light of street lamps.

"But if my sister doesn't like me, she shouldn't stay with us," Helen continued. "There are a hundred people in New York who would put her up."

Turning left onto Eighty-Second, the car swung wide in the snow. Oliver straightened out before trading the street for the sidewalk.

"But I have to tell you—"

"Yes. What is it, Helen?" Oliver had pulled up outside a parking lot. The metal gate was down.

"When I said that Ella and I had spoken about her being late to pick up Rebecca and that she did not apologize, what I meant to tell you was that she's taken her things and left."

Oliver pressed the horn to alert the attendant. "What are you talking about?"

"She's gone."

"Did she have any money?"

"I wouldn't know. I didn't tell her to leave. She said she felt unwelcome, and I agreed with her that she wasn't. That's it."

Oliver hit his horn again, searching through the windshield for signs of an attendant. When no one came, he said to her, "I can't talk about this," and he got out of the BMW and tottered up to the metal gate. Cars were parked all the way to the entrance. Through a doorway at the back, the crossed legs of a seated man were visible. Oliver rang the bell. The man didn't move.

"Are you dead in there!" he shouted.

But the attendant remained perfectly still in his chair.

Oliver returned to the car, slamming the door shut. In the leather driver's seat, he said, "It's probably the same everywhere."

"You'll find something," Helen said.

However, the next lots were full. They rode past their old spot. Now it was occupied. When the fuel light went on, Oliver couldn't help himself. He grabbed his wife by the shoulders and shook her. "Why did I let you talk me into this!"

"Oh, let go of me, Oliver!"

"This is your fault!"

"We had to move the car."

"No, we didn't."

"We were just going to leave it in the snow?"

"Yes!"

Helen pulled away from her husband. Everyone was silent. The car rumbled past building canopies flapping hard in the wind. White snow dervishes swirled down the avenue. Rebecca gazed at them while they spun away, her hand pressed to the window.

All of a sudden, Helen was saying, "And do you know before Ella left tonight, I told her, I went, 'I've tried to do everything I can for you, but you take advantage of me and I'm done with it.' And she said, 'I take advantage of you? I take advantage! How could you say I take advantage?' I mean, does she have no sense of what she is? But then I know she does, Oliver. That's the thing. Which means it's an act. Can you imagine that? An act!"

Making a right turn onto their block, Oliver was prepared to tell Helen to get out and take their daughter with her, he would look for parking alone. But then a miracle—a spot had opened up right in front of their building.

"Holy shit. Look at that!" Oliver pulled between two snow-clad cars. He was out on the street before Helen and Rebecca had unbuckled their seatbelts. "Come on, you two!" he shouted.

Helen looked grimly at her husband. "Will you wait a second!"

But Oliver was knee-deep in snow, and furious. He said, "Forget it. I'll meet you both upstairs," and he rushed off between the large double doors.

A moment later, Helen and Rebecca confronted the startling warmth of the lobby. Observing the puddles on the marble floor, Helen asked the doorman Edmond, who would have to mop now, if Oliver was responsible for these wet tracks.

"Yes," Edmond said.

"I thought so," replied Helen. She apologized on behalf of her husband. Then she told the doorman that Oliver would need to borrow a shovel in the morning to get the car out. And would one be available at eight? She knew the doormen shoveled the sidewalk mornings and, with snow like this, there was no question there'd be plenty to remove.

Edmond said, "Not a problem, Helen."

"It'll be available to him?"

"Yes."

Rebecca followed her mother toward the elevator at the end of the lobby. But Helen suddenly checked inside the door to the stairwell. She looked up to the second landing, and said to her daughter, "I thought Ella might be asleep there. You think she's in the storage room, maybe?"

"I don't think so, Mom."

Helen's back straightened. She called out to Edmond and asked him whether he'd seen Ella leave that evening. He said he had.

"Around 6 p.m.?"

"Probably six, yeah."

"She hasn't come back, has she?"

"No."

Helen told Edmond that, should her sister return, he had to ring up before letting her in. The doorman lifted his hat and said he would. Then, pressing for the elevator, Helen reminded her daughter how her sister had plenty of friends around the city. She wouldn't be sleeping on the streets. She would find a warm bed tonight, a cup of peppermint tea, a loan for tomorrow and the day after that. She said to her daughter, "You have to watch out for people. They will try to squeeze everything out of you—" Then she grabbed Rebecca by the arm roughly, and pulled her inside the elevator.

IX. IN-COMING

Oliver hadn't seen his wife Sheila in six months. But she was now aboard a red-eye from Los Angeles to New York. And how long would she be staying? What had she told him? Two weeks? Less, maybe?

These days, Oliver and Sheila spoke by phone every few hours. All conversations centered on the business of the lawsuit. What was the key to winning? How could they prove Doris had forced Eliza to sign the new will? Sheila couldn't talk about any of it without skidding off into rage. She cursed and accused, made predictions and threats. It exhausted Oliver. In fact, days before Sheila's arrival in New York, he became sick. His stomach wasn't right. He was nauseous. He stayed in bed and slept, didn't go outside. He thought he should see a doctor. He hadn't had a physical in years. He would go, except he was so tired he didn't think he could make it uptown to his physician's.

Then, that morning, Sheila called Oliver just minutes after landing at JFK, and once he was off the phone he was suddenly up and hurrying around the apartment, straightening and dusting, throwing away weeks-old takeout containers from the refrigerator, cleaning the toilet and putting fresh sheets on the bed. For three days he'd been unable to move, and now he couldn't sit still. He was adjusting curtains when his wife knocked at the door. He let her in, and Sheila stepped right past her husband into the apartment. Pushing two large suitcases against a wall, she collapsed onto the sofa and began complaining about the state of airplane food.

"Worse than ever *and* it costs you."

"Let me make you something. You want some eggs?"

"How about Egg Beaters?"

"I can separate the whites."

"You have plain yogurt?"

"I can go out and buy some."

"That's not necessary."

"You should have everything you need. I'll go get yogurt. What else would you like? I can't believe I didn't do a shop."

"You don't have to. I'm not even hungry." Sheila massaged her scalp, her anxiety playing out through half-closed blue eyes. "I called Jerome five times. He won't get back to me."

Looking under the coffee table for his shoes, Oliver said, "Uh-huh."

"I need to be in touch with him."

"You will be."

"His testimony is everything."

"I know, Sheila."

"And I called Violet's apartment and spoke with her daughter. Seems she's flown home to Jamaica and has no plans of returning anytime soon. As far as witnesses, that only leaves us Jerome. You've got to call Rebecca. We need her help. She's friendly with him, right?"

"Who's friendly with who?" Oliver asked.

"Your daughter, Rebecca, is friendly with Jerome."

"I know. So what?"

"So we'll ask her to help us with Jerome."

"Oh, yeah. We can do that."

Oliver appeared distracted. As it was, he was remembering a very strange incident. During his last two weeks at the loft—late at night, unable to sleep—he'd gone to have a bite of chicken in the kitchen when he'd heard noises coming from his father's studio, the light tap of a hammer and then the sound of someone speaking to himself. Oliver had gone to look, but he'd been unable to get into the studio. The doorway had been blocked by a refrigerator.

"So I call out. I say, 'Is anyone in there?' And it's Jerome."

"Jerome?"

"Yes. And he tells me not to worry. He's just doing a little work."

"What?"

"Well, and I was so out of it, I didn't know if it was really him or if I was imagining things."

"Then what happened?"

"Nothing. That was it. I went back to bed."

Sheila shook her hands in the air, and at once she began to shout at her husband. She couldn't believe it—why hadn't he told her about this before? Was he a moron? Jerome had been there to steal.

"No wonder he's not returning my calls. He's afraid. He thinks we're onto him."

"I'm sure you're wrong."

"Oh you're sure, are you? How well do you know Jerome? Have you ever been to his apartment? Have you met his family, his friends? What's his last name?"

Oliver tried to remember. He couldn't. "He was working."

"Working? What would he be working on?"

"I have no idea."

Sheila waved Oliver off with a sweep of her arm.

Oliver said, "You know what, I'll go get those egg whites. You're tired. Take a nap. I'll be back soon."

And he left the apartment. He felt instantly set free. Had he been breathing the last ten minutes? His heart rate was returning to normal now. But his wife should sleep. What would he do? For weeks he had been meaning to go look in on Laura Saks.

His ex-fiancée welcomed him into her Columbus Avenue apartment. In the living room, a bottle of white wine was open on the table. The dogs were at the daycare on Seventy-Fourth. Laura's tan-colored dress was one that Oliver had bought her twenty years before. It was long and slimming, a little fancy for the occasion. But Oliver had come without giving much notice. He apologized.

"My wife just got to town. I needed a little space."

Laura liked that. She leaned back on the sofa, her upper lip rising to reveal dark pink gums. Her brown hair was damp and held back in a white elastic band, which she adjusted twice before taking up her wineglass and toasting.

"To an afternoon of leisure."

"Yes," Oliver said. "To that."

His wife had drained him, and it showed. Oliver sat in a chair with his legs stuck out straight and his body lifeless. "You're good to take me in."

"That's what old friends do."

Oliver flashed her a grin. He was at ease in Laura's company, and in this apartment where he had spent so many nights. Nothing had changed here except for the hallways outside the front door, which had been given a makeover to match the rise in the economy.

"So your wife," Laura was saying, her legs crossed and body slanted across the sofa, "she showed up and you took off."

"Yes. She came in the door from the airport, and she hadn't sat down before she was going on and on about the lawsuit. It's all she wants talks about. I mean, how about a kiss hello? Maybe she asks me how I'm doing. We talk about where we'll have dinner tonight, where we'll walk, what we'll see. But I get none of that."

Laura smiled through pursed lips while her small shoulders dipped inward. Oh, she knew just what he meant. Two months before, Sheila had emailed her.

"She did?"

"Yes, Oliver, you gave her my email."

"It's hard to remember much these days."

Well, she forgave him for giving out her personal contact information without asking first. But he should be aware, he'd sent Laura down a difficult road. What had Sheila wanted? Just to know if Laura had ever seen Doris do anything in the past that a judge would find interesting. Something cruel or perverse.

"And I tell her I'll think about it. But by the next day, Sheila's sent me a new email. This one's about Ben. Surely, in all my years of knowing him, I've seen your dad take a pool cue to one of you or bump a driver on the LIE. I tell her I'll think about that, too. But then two, maybe three minutes later, I get a third email. Now she's asking about you and your mother. Would I be willing to go before a grand jury and discuss how you two had been as close as a mother and son could be? Would I talk about how good Eliza had been to you? How much she had loved her only son? I started receiving a new email every day. She didn't let up for weeks."

"I'm sorry."

"Well, I want to help. But she's so abrasive."

"That same person is in my apartment. I have to go back there and deal with her."

"And she won't give you a kiss hello."

"Not one."

"She won't want to have any fun, either."

"No fun."

"Just work, and work, and work, Oliver."

"That's right, Laura," he said. Then, screwing up one side of his face, he asked Laura if he could go into her bedroom and take a nap. "I'm so wiped."

"Oh, sure. Of course," Laura said, surprised by the request. "Just give me a minute to change the sheets."

"No," Oliver said, "I don't care about the sheets. But would you wake me in an hour? I shouldn't be away any longer than that."

Laura nodded. "One hour. You got it."

At noon, Laura woke Oliver. He took a taxi back to his neighborhood. At the Food Emporium, he bought Egg Beaters, yogurt, a whole chicken, skim milk, and a box of chocolate donuts. He picked up a regular coffee and a buttered bagel for his doorman, checked the mailbox, and thought how good it was that Sheila had had a rest. He, too, was feeling more awake.

He stuck his key in the lock. The door was open. He would have to remind his wife that this was New York City and that he knew stories, stories he would rather not repeat but would be forced to if she didn't start locking the front door. He hung his jacket on the stand. He called out to Sheila, but she didn't answer. Was she still asleep?

But then, what in God's name was this? For a moment, Oliver felt a sort of relapse of the symptoms he'd been experiencing in the days before Sheila's arrival. That total loss of energy, the nausea. He stared out at the living room. Stacks of papers were everywhere, forming neat piles, some very tall. They were labeled with index cards: "Original Will," "New Will," "Doris," "Sondra," "Ben," "Eliza," "Jerome," "Lawyers," "SoHo," "Southampton." A fax machine was on the floor, spitting out paper. Next to it was a narrow wooden table with a brand-new desktop computer on top. A dry-erase board with the words HOW TO WIN THE CASE written on it in red marker hung from the wall.

Suddenly, the front door slammed. Sheila came walking in with a large box in her arms. She dropped it on a chair and heaved. "Thing weighs a ton," she said.

"What the hell is that?"

"It's a printer. It was on sale."

Oliver looked for a place to sit down and gather his thoughts, but even the couch was covered in papers. He said, "What have you done to my apartment?"

"You don't like it?"

"Like it? It looks like a war room."

"It is a war room." Sheila was busting the printer out of its box. By the looks of her, she relished the feeling of ripping open cardboard.

"These wires! Why are there so many?"

"We'll cover up the wires."

"How long was I even gone?" Oliver looked at his watch. "Four hours? You did all this in four hours?"

"This is just the beginning, Oliver. Three file cabinets are being delivered tomorrow. And I got you a desk of your own. I've been thinking about our diet, too. No more dairy or carbs. I've got to find someone to play racquetball with. You should start running. We've got to get our energy up. If we see every part of our lives, every action, every decision, as affecting the outcome of the lawsuit, if we can get ourselves to that place, there's no chance we lose."

Out the window, Oliver saw the Morgan Library, where J.P. had lived. He said, "I know I've come down in the world, Sheila, but it doesn't mean I have to live in a goddamn office."

"Oh, please, Oliver. Forget how you once had it. Since selling my house, I've been living in a motel. I can't even afford a hotel. How do you think that feels? I'm sixty-three and I don't know how I'll pay for the rest of my life. But that's the past. We've got a lawsuit to win."

"I know we do."

"And if you think it'll just happen without us putting everything we've got into it, then you're wrong."

"I understand."

"Good. Now come on already. Focus."

They went to work. Sheila spent her days reading through documents and taking notes. The fax machine was going twenty-four-seven. Oliver felt unsure of his role. Afraid that he was interrupting his wife, he would ask her what he should be doing. She would assign him tasks:

"Take these papers and organize them chronologically." "Put the blue pens with the blue pens and the black pens with the black and the red pens with the pens. I need them separated. It's essential for my underlining." "Go out and get us two turkey sandwiches with lettuce and tomato from the deli, no cheese and no mayo, and some espresso shots from the Italian bakery."

They were menial jobs, which never took Oliver more than an hour. Then he'd have to go back to Sheila and ask her what he should be doing now. Most the time, Sheila would hum, and her eyes would roll into the corners, and she'd say, "Take a little break. Ten minutes and I'll have you going again." It seemed like she would prefer to do the work on her own. At times, Oliver considered asking his wife if he should even be there. He was probably just slowing her down. But then, he didn't want her to think he wasn't invested, or that he'd rather be someplace else. In the afternoons, he would tell Sheila that he was going up to Central Park to run, and instead he would visit Laura's apartment and drink wine and reminisce. Why hadn't it worked out for them? They had been close so many times.

"I fell out of love," Oliver told her.

"So you slept with that Mandy."

"Things were already over between us by that time. You suffocated the air out of the relationship. You were on top of me at every second. Now, look at my marriage to Sheila."

"What about it?"

"We live three thousand miles apart. That works out very well for us."

"But you don't like to be around her."

"Not true. I love her from a distance."

Snorting, Laura rose in her white robe and went to retrieve a second bottle of wine from the kitchen. She talked from the other room. Why, if Oliver had shown more confidence in her, she would have made him happy. He destroyed her self-esteem. It was his fault that she couldn't give him the space he needed.

"I take some responsibility."

"And I felt used. I was supporting you all those years."

"How much do I owe you? I think I brought my checkbook." Oliver was wearing black, pocketless running shorts and a torn red T-shirt. There was a ten-dollar bill stuck behind his headband.

"Oh, I don't know, a few hundred thousand."

"That much? God, that is a lot."

"Well, how much do you have?"

"Maybe two thousand."

"No, that's not going to cut it."

Afterward, Oliver would return home and be given tasks straightaway. These pages had to be photocopied, there was a shop up the street that charged only five cents a copy, he should make sure to paperclip each set of pages. He should pick up a three-ringed hole puncher, too. And some more pens. She didn't mind it if he spent a little extra on a pen that actually worked. She demonstrated for him. Did he see, these pens were crap. It looked like they had ink, but they didn't. She could also use a stronger coffee bean. The supermarket brands might have been all right for his father, but times had changed. After a single cup her hands should be shaking. And could he buy fruit that wasn't so ripe?

"Thanks."

On occasion, Laura would come down to Oliver's neighborhood and accompany him on his errands. They would end up in a restaurant.

"I've been telling my wife that I've been exercising over these last weeks, but I think I've put on ten pounds."

"Good. You're too skinny."

"It's Sheila. Being around her takes weight off a person."

"What is the latest news?"

"About the case?"

"Yes, the case."

"I don't know. But I should ask my wife, shouldn't I?"

Back home and inquiring about the lawsuit, Sheila had very little information. "It's moving along," she told him. "It's such a slow process."

Yes, he told her. That's what he thought she'd say. But was there anything more she wanted him to do? Nothing? Okay, then he was going for a run in Central Park.

A half-hour later, uptown on Columbus, his ex-fiancée was suggesting that they not drink white wine this afternoon. She was sick of the stuff. How about a gimlet? The roof of the building was outfitted with a patio. They brought their cocktails upstairs and reclined on chaises. Oliver said he would feel guilty for shirking his work, but Sheila had made it clear to him that he wasn't needed.

"She treats you like you're an idiot. It isn't right."

"I appreciate that, honey."

"You're not there just to make photocopies and do the shopping. She should make real use of you."

"It's nice to hear you say it, Laura."

The next day, Sheila sent Oliver to the New York Public Library. She wanted him to find press pieces on *Shout!* Oliver had always said that Doris had put herself at the center of their media coverage, and Sheila would like to paint the picture of a woman desperate for credit and attention. Oliver thought it was a good idea, too. But the library was a mystery to him. The archives had been digitized. And yet how did the new system work? And was there anyone in the library who could help him? He was gone from the apartment eight hours, and four were spent at the library in utter confusion. The rest of the time he was at Laura's, bemoaning his trials.

"What do I look like, a research assistant? I spent my youth in nightclubs, listening to music."

"So what did you find?"

"A couple of articles. Sheila won't be satisfied, I can tell you that much."

And she wasn't. Four pieces? That was all he'd come up with? How was it possible? There must be hundreds of articles out there. He had to try again, and do better. Oliver apologized. He said he didn't feel comfortable in a library. Maybe Sheila should do that work herself. He would be happy to read through anything she found and underline the relevant passages.

But then Sheila kicked him off the job. Told him to go out and get her a tuna wrap with a sour pickle.

"She doesn't have any patience with me. It's insulting."

"Don't take it so hard," Laura told him. "She's under a lot of pressure."

"So am I."

"Of course you are. But you deal better with stress."

Oliver accepted that. Then he clapped his hands, applauding Laura's lasagna. It was delicious. And the garlic bread was out of this world. She had never cooked for him this way when they'd been together.

"I went to culinary school after we broke up. I had to do something to get out of my head. You remember how bad things were for me."

"Well, they taught you well."

Oliver went home with a full stomach. Sheila was on the floor in the living room, doing pushups. She told him to drop down beside her and do fifty of his own.

"That's not possible. I'm stuffed."

"You already ate?"

"After my run in the park, I was famished. I had a cheeseburger."

Sheila didn't ask for more details. She put a laundry bag in Oliver's arms. He should take it down to the basement and run a cycle of clothes.

"Can I sit first?"

"Okay. But if you're going to get everything cleaned and folded and put away in the drawers before bedtime, I suggest you do it now."

So, a moment later, Oliver went down to the laundry room. He had to get his wife out of New York. No, she couldn't stay. Not if he was to live. When was the last time he'd slept past 8 a.m.? Sheila wouldn't let him. Every morning it was, "Up, up, up. Come on. We've got work to do." And then, thirty minutes later, she'd have him out on the sidewalk with a to-do list. He'd had enough. He would bring it up with her tomorrow. He would tell her that he needed a break, and that she should go home to L.A.

And yet the next morning, when Oliver woke, Sheila was gone. There was no note. She wasn't answering her phone. What time was it, anyway? 10 a.m.? Oh, joy. He opened the shades and brewed a pot of coffee and scrambled eggs. This was the way it was meant to be. He took a long shower. He dried off in the bed beside an open window, gazing down at the McKim Building. Maybe he'd read a book. Or a magazine. Or how about a little television? But a moment later, Oliver got to his feet. He wanted to be out in the world.

He called Laura and asked her to meet him in an hour at Penn Station. Where were they going? That was a surprise, he said. They got on a Long Island Railroad. The train car was empty on a Thursday morning in September. They drank coffee out of paper cups, split a bagel, read the *New York Post*, played gin rummy. The train pulled into Southampton at twenty after one. They got into a taxi parked outside the station. The driver complimented them on picking such a gorgeous day to come out to the beach. Minutes later, the car pulled up in front of the Arkin house. Oliver paid with a twenty, and the car skidded away. The front door of the house was locked, but Oliver found the extra set of keys under the rock near the juniper tree at the foot of the steps. The alarm sounded when the door opened. Oliver knew the code: 0913. His father's birthday. It surprised him that the lights went on when he hit the switch. He'd figured the bills had been going unpaid and that the power would have been cut. Everything was very clean. It smelled like Pinesol. The domed skylight above the living room, cracked for years, had been replaced. The glass dining table where his father had sat reading and taking notes was now a wooden farm table with benches for seats. There was the swimming pool, visible through two large sliding doors. It had been covered with a green tarp for the last five years of his parents' lives. His parents had had no interest in swimming, and with the grandchildren grown, they'd seen no reason to pay for the upkeep. So why was the cover off, the water treated and clean of leaves and debris? They decided Doris was renting out the house and taking cash on the side, and that Oliver would have to nail her for this.

Next, they found old swimsuits in a dresser. The water in the pool was cold but revivifying. Laura said Oliver's hair was too long and she would give him a trim. Offered to get rid of the beard, too. She preferred his face shaven. He looked old. Oliver kicked hard at the water. Rotating like a seal, he gazed at her with a half-serious, half-mocking expression, told her he liked his hair and beard as they were and, in time, she would learn to do the same. More importantly, what were they going to do about food? They should have a long lunch.

They toweled off on the deck, got back in their clothes, and walked into town. Laura wanted lobsters and caviar and champagne. Oliver knew just the place. Their table was outdoors on a red brick patio enclosed by cypresses. The waiter over-poured Laura's glass, spilling champagne. She said it was okay. However, the sun was shining so strongly here, and did he mind putting up an umbrella? Now shaded, they were comfortable. So how many pounds should their lobsters weigh? Two and a half? Three? The food took a long time to come out. But that, too, was okay. They were in no rush. Oliver cracked Laura's shells, poked his forefinger through the leg joints and pushed out the meat. The butter ran down their arms. Greasy fingerprints marked their champagne flutes. Oliver thought the second bottle of champagne was probably a mistake, but Laura wasn't of the same opinion. They would sober up in the ocean afterward. And what did it matter if they didn't? A day trip like this deserved a lot of drink.

An hour later, Laura paid the tab with four one-hundred-dollar bills. At the beach, the sand burned their feet. Their bathing suits were back at the house, but they stood in ankle-deep water with their arms around each other's waists and their eyes set on a large vessel moving across the horizon. They expressed their wish for night. In the dark, they could take off their clothes and get in the water. That wasn't possible just now. There were people everywhere.

When they got back to the house, it was 5:30 p.m. They spent time in the basement looking through old things. Eliza's clothes were zipped up in plastic garment bags and hanging on racks. There were vases and lamps, lucite folding chairs, chandeliers, Art Nouveau screens, photo albums, doors, books, and boxes full of door knobs. Laura was holding a framed photograph of Oliver's parents from the winter of 1960. Eliza wore a black mink coat. Ben was in a black pinstriped suit, smoking a cigar.

"The power couple."

Oliver took the frame from Laura's hands, staring. "This man."

"I was so afraid of him," Laura said, releasing a short, high-pitched laugh.

"Who wasn't?"

"What about Rebecca? Ben loved her. She had nothing to fear."

"I'm not sure she sees it that way."

"How does she see it, Oliver?" But before he could answer, Laura said, "I would ask her myself, but she doesn't return any of my calls."

A light chain hung between them. Oliver could feel the heat coming off the uncovered bulb overhead. He positioned the photo of Eliza and Ben under his arm, looking Laura in the eyes. He said, "She's as busy as the mayor."

"It's more than that. She's angry with me. She's cut me off. You know, you put so much time in with a person—and for what? They don't care. They'll just use you and throw you out."

"Rebecca was a child when you knew her."

"Fourteen by the end. For a girl, that's old enough to know everything."

Oliver shook his head. "Give her a break."

"All right. I'm just telling you how it is."

Now Oliver was saying that they should get going. Their train back to New York was in forty minutes. It would be trouble if they missed it. The next train wouldn't get them back to the city until after 10 p.m., and Sheila would want to know where he had been.

"I thought we were going to put our suits on and go for a swim in the ocean."

"Sorry, Laura. We're out of time."

"You don't want to try and do it quickly?"

"No. I'm all clean and dressed. We'll do it another day."

A half hour later, their taxi was pulling up in front of the train station. Only four people were waiting on the platform. Oliver bought tickets at the kiosk. Suddenly Laura was apologizing. She hadn't meant to blame Rebecca for what had happened between them. Could he just forget about it so that they could enjoy the rest of their time together?

The train was coming now. Oliver took Laura's hand. "Of course," he said.

Laura kissed a spot on his face just to the left of his nose. At one time in their lives she had made a point of kissing him there often. She pushed her head against his shoulder, and said, "Thank you, Oliver."

X. TRUST

That same Thursday morning in September, Rebecca woke at 5 a.m. She had taken her old red ten-speed Peugeot out of storage the week before and had been biking early in the day or late at night, when there were fewer cars on the road. Riding now on the gold coast of Fifth Avenue, where the Plaza and Tiffany's and Trump Towers came and went from view, she could feel the unevenness of the pavement through the handlebars. The sky was gray. Mornings like these reminded Rebecca that New York was a city on the water. Damp and cool, with seagulls circling above and the light fog hovering over black streets— she changed gears, looking for more resistance, the bike chain making the sound of a funicular going up rails. She was panting hard, digging past St. Patrick's. Her vision seemed exceptionally sharp, her arms full of strength. On Forty-Ninth, she made a right turn, heading through Rockefeller Center, her legs pumping quickly. Then she pulled over in front of Radio City. Her phone was ringing. It was Sheila. She didn't answer, but went into the park at Central Park South, took the loop all the way past Lasker Rink, where the road inclined sharply, and back down the West Side, exiting onto Seventy-Seventh Street at the Natural History Museum. She walked her bike the last last two blocks home. Stepping off the elevator onto the sixth floor, she saw Gertrude Fish standing in front of her door in a black bathrobe, smoking a cigarette, her hand pressed to her head. She was reading a notice from the building. There was one on every doormat. Rebecca had never seen Gertrude at this hour. Her dark eyes wanted no part of the light. Her back was hunched over dramatically. But now she looked up at Rebecca and pointed. "You've got a post-coital glow."

"I was biking."

"Hmm. You must be parched. How about a glass of wine?"

"It's seven in the morning, Gertrude."

"When you hear what this letter says, you'll need a drink, too."

Gertrude led Rebecca inside her apartment, and to the kitchen table where tea steeped in a red ceramic pot. Gertrude pushed the pot aside, uncorked a bottle of red wine, and poured two glasses, forcing one into Rebecca's hand.

"No, thank you," she said.

Gertrude's cheeks filled with air, and her eyes seemed to expand to a point of bursting. She said, "You've got all this gray in your hair. Is this the look you're going for?"

"Gertrude."

"What, you think hair color isn't important? The last time I saw you, you were thirty-five. Now you look thirty-six. Did you have a birthday?"

"No. I didn't."

"My point exactly." Gertrude stuck a finger in her ear and began scratching there. She said, "I've lost, Rebecca."

"You've what?"

"They're pushing me out of the building."

"Who is?"

"They are!"

It was like this: Each of the four penthouse apartments in the building had been experiencing leaky ceilings for years, and the time had come to renovate the roof. Although this affected only those people living in one of the four penthouses, according to the co-op board, it was everyone's roof and the responsibility of payment would be distributed throughout each unit. The board presidents had brought in a number of contractors and the bidding had been highly competitive. The cost of the job seemed extremely fair. What did this mean for the individual tenant? A doubling of the monthly maintenance bill for the next two years, effective immediately.

"That's sixteen hundred more dollars a month!"

"What? Why haven't I heard anything about this until now?"

"Because, Rebecca, you've had your head up your ass. They've been going on about it for almost a year. But I never thought it would come to this. I can't afford that kind of increase. I'll have to sell my apartment and move out of the city. Where will I go? Eastern Pennsylvania? Maine? I knew a man in Flanders once who wanted to marry me. This was thirty years ago. I doubt he's still alive, but if he is, I'll tell him I'm ready to accept his proposal."

Rebecca put down her wine glass and fixed herself a cup of tea. An extra sixteen hundred dollars a month over the next two years for a new roof was preposterous, but it wouldn't kill her. Her end-of-the-year bonus alone would more than take care of the expense. She apologized to Gertrude. She told her to keep up hope. "It could work itself out."

"Bullshit it will. They've won."

"You're still here. Something could happen."

"Like what?"

"Like a commission."

"Not likely."

"I could lend you money."

"Lend me money?"

"You'll pay me back."

"No, no, I don't borrow money."

"You could stay in your home."

"No. No."

"Just this one time."

"I'd rather die."

"You've got so much stuff, getting out of here might actually kill you."

"Not true. I'm tougher than that."

"Why don't you think about it?"

But no, Rebecca wasn't listening. Gertrude had already made up her mind. She would sell her apartment, pick a new town, and move there. "Everyone in the building will be celebrating. 'Oh, we finally dumped her. Property values are going to soar.' I swear, these people disgust me."

"I'm sorry about this, Gertrude. I have to get ready for work now. Let me know. The offer stands."

Rebecca said goodbye and went down the hall to her apartment. Her stepmother had called two more times in the last hour. What could she possibly want? Rebecca wouldn't think about it. She showered, dressed, and left for work. But coming into the office at a quarter to nine, her secretary stopped her. There was a message from Sheila. Rebecca should call her right away. It was urgent.

Rebecca closed her door and dialed her stepmother. The moment Sheila answered, Rebecca apologized for not having called sooner. She said she'd had a busy morning. So what was going on? Was she all right?

"I have to see you, Rebecca."

"Why?"

"We'll talk about it in person. Can you come over today at three?"

"Come over? Could you meet me near my office?"

"No. All the papers for the lawsuit are here. I need to show them to you."

Rebecca acquiesced. Then she asked if her father would be joining them. But Sheila didn't answer. She said, "I'll see you then," and hung up.

A feeling of regret seized Rebecca the moment she got off. She had spoken to herself about it too many times: she wouldn't make appointments with anyone she didn't want to see. A simple rule. And she had just broken it. Rebecca leaned hard to one side of her chair, grimacing. Her whole day was ruined now. How would she get her work done? She had phone calls to make, documents to read. But she had been robbed of her energy.

A minute later, Rebecca got up from her desk and left the office. She went uptown to Café Sabarsky. The restaurant's décor reminded her that she didn't have to leave the city to feel transported to a faraway place and time. Between the chandeliers and tremendous mirrored walls, the selection of international newspapers hanging on wooden rods like drying laundry just behind the grand piano—*Le Monde, Der Spiegel, el Dais*—it all had the effect of sending her over the Atlantic. She sensed her anonymity acutely and was pleased. Her spirits were lifting. She was seated at one of the marble-topped café tables in the busy dining room, drinking a glass of red wine. Surrounded by so many tourists, she let herself believe that she was in the city of those who dined around her, and not the other way around. Yes—and she imagined that she was feeling more at ease now than she had all day. She flipped open the thick black menu. Perhaps goulash or a bratwurst, then a strudel. She would like a feast.

On occasion, Rebecca wondered what she looked like to a person who saw her out in the world. Inspecting produce in a grocery store, hailing a cab—what impression did she give off to a stranger? Whatever the answer, she concluded that anyone who saw this young couple seated in front of her would have to think they were very much in love. And what about this man bursting through the café entrance, the strain of a difficult subway commute there in his expression? And this teenage girl hiding from her parents between the upturned collar of her shirt and her knuckles set beneath her chin. Rebecca liked them all.

There was a postcard on the table advertising a cabaret performance the following week, and she thought she would come back and see it. Or perhaps she would get on a plane and go to Vienna. When was the last time she had gone anywhere? Years. But where could she go from here to have more of a foreign land? After finishing her goulash, Rebecca decided on the Oyster Bar. The restaurant had always reminded her of the kind of place Londoners might have taken shelter during a German bomb raid, but with more charming lighting. She'd been many times. However, once inside Grand Central, she couldn't find the entrance. Was it closer to Lexington or Vanderbilt? Which ramp did you follow down? There was a back door, but where was that? She let herself drift onto a platform and stood between two trains, both heading upriver to the Hudson Valley. Conductors in navy uniforms were gathered there. One shouted above the din of the silver machines, asking her where to. Regarding their heavy gray faces, the overworked eyes, she didn't say. That they were trying to be helpful didn't change the fact that they were being nuisances. She wished to be left alone. She turned her back to the conductors, waiting for the quiet feeling of loss which would come when the trains pulled out of the station. However, Rebecca left the platform before either train.

She got directions to the restaurant from a shoe shiner. She went right up to the bar, where it reeked of booze, and told the bartender, "Beefeaters, up, extra olives." But at the next moment, seeing that Sheila had texted asking where she was, she left the restaurant. One half of the sidewalk was cordoned off for the purpose of construction, and she walked single file in a crowded lane beside an office building, pressing herself to sense the sound and taste of the ocean. The farther she got from the restaurant, the harder this became. But then, across the street from her father's apartment, with the McKim Building—why, here was Rome. At the entryway to the library, she hung her hands on the chest-high, green oxidized metal gate, looking in. And she was there, near the Tevere, and the Villa Borghese, not far from the Vatican. This was the trip she'd been meaning to go on. At last, she had made the time, and taken a grand shortcut, saving more hours than she had to spare. Why did it all seem better now? Painless yet vivid, delicious, *adagio*. She would stay. She desperately wanted to remain. But then she had to go upstairs.

And once inside her father's apartment, the fantasy was over. There was Sheila, explaining how the legal documents were organized, starting with the file cabinet in the living room, then the accordion files in the kitchen, and lastly the binders on the shelf in the bedroom. Rebecca should pay attention to every last word she was saying. Perhaps she wanted to take notes. Regardless, she should speak to the lawyers as soon as possible and be brought up to date on her father's legal affairs, because Sheila was done. In fact, there was a half-packed suitcase open on the floor in the bedroom, and she was collecting her toiletries in a large ziplock bag.

"Your father doesn't care about the lawsuit, and I can't make him care. I've tried."

"So you're leaving?"

"Yes. Back to Los Angeles."

Sheila was pulling open all the drawers. Here was a pair of socks, a shirt, a bracelet. She dumped it all into the suitcase. She said she didn't have much time. Her plane departed in three hours.

"Is my father okay with you leaving?"

"Yes, Rebecca. He wants me out of his hair."

Rebecca had been clutching her purse to her body. But now her arm floated out in front of her, and she asked if Sheila and her father would divorce. Sheila's answer came slowly. She said that sounded difficult and expensive. For now, they would take some time apart, a few months at most. Although who knew, perhaps a longer separation would be necessary. It had been a while since Sheila had thought about her own life. She was ready to start.

"Rebecca, you'll see firsthand how this lawsuit can drain you of all your time and energy."

"You think I'm taking over for you, is that it?"

"It's that or you can kiss your father's inheritance good-bye." She said Oliver would never follow through on the lawsuit without someone pushing him to the finish. Rebecca was the only candidate for the job. Unless she could think of someone else. "But of course you can't, because there's no one but you now."

Rebecca shook her head. She said, "What about the lawyers? Can't they handle everything?"

"No," Sheila answered, "they can't."

"Why not?"

"There's a hundred reasons why."

"Are they incompetent?"

"No."

"So what, then?"

"Take Jerome. He was with your grandparents when the new wills were signed. And he needs to be convinced to testify. But the lawyers can't even get him on the phone. You probably could. You're friends. He would listen to you."

Rebecca's head dropped forward onto her fingertips. She told her stepmother that she could be disbarred for meddling that way.

"Think of it as a calculated risk. If your father doesn't get his inheritance, how will he survive? He has no money."

"I'm sure there's a smarter way to go about it."

"Well, you're the lawyer. If anyone can figure it out, it's you."

Rebecca's gaze moved around the bedroom. She said, "Where is my father, anyway?"

"Honestly, I don't know. I've already tried him three times. He doesn't answer."

"Should we be worried?"

"Worried? Rebecca, this is what he does! Just yesterday he told me he was going out to get staples, and he didn't come back for six hours. That's when I realized I couldn't do this anymore."

Rebecca brought her hand to the side of her head. To alleviate the pain behind her eyes, she went into the medicine cabinet in the bathroom and took an aspirin. She drank from the faucet and dried her face on her forearm. She returned to the bedroom. Sheila was on her knees, zipping up the suitcase. Rebecca thanked her. "You've done a lot for my father."

"Yes. And now it's your turn, Rebecca. With a case like this, you'll have to be creative. Doris's lawyers are very good."

"Well, I haven't committed to anything."

"Don't be coy. This is your case to win now."

"Not true."

"Then let your dad go to the poor house."

"The poor house?"

"He's got nothing."

"I know."

"You do? You don't act like it."

"All right, Sheila. I have to leave. You have a nice flight."

Rebecca let herself out. She took the stairs down. In the lobby, she stood before a mirror and brushed her hair. Were her eyes bloodshot? She took a step closer to the mirror and saw that they were, yes. Maybe it was because of the martini? Perhaps lack of sleep? Or Sheila? That was it. Her stepmother's mouth, a force of nature, which would not stop with its assumptions and its demands, had caused the blood vessels in her eyes to burst. She reached into her purse for her sunglasses. Raul, the doorman, asked her where she was heading now.

"Back to the office," she said.

"You know, you look a little under the weather."

"Oh?" Rebecca touched her face. So everyone could tell. How bad was it?

"Maybe you want to get a juice on the way," the doorman said. Then he went to open the front door. A woman entered the building. "Ms. Sears, how are you?"

"Hello, Raul. Take these."

The woman pushed her shopping bags into Raul's hands. Rebecca saw the woman in the reflection of the mirror. She thought she was the image of Marilyn Monroe, if the actress had lived another thirty years and never cleaned up. The face was attractive but bloated, the curled platinum blond hair badly damaged. The skirt and blouse were meant for someone a third her age. She walked straight past Rebecca. And once Rebecca saw her blue wide-set eyes, she recognized her instantly.

"It's Mandy Sears," she said, quietly, to herself.

Rebecca had never liked Mandy, but she wouldn't pretend as if she had ever given her father's ex-lover a chance. Although, why was she here now?

Suddenly, Rebecca turned toward her and said, "You're Mandy Sears, aren't you?"

Mandy had stepped onto the elevator. She acknowledged Rebecca with a suspicious look. "I am. Who are you?"

"Rebecca Arkin, Oliver's daughter."

"Ohhhhh, yes. Nice to see you."

Rebecca drew her forefinger down one side of her nose and then the other, trying to make quick sense of the situation.

Raul had taken out a broom and was sweeping up near the front door. However, Rebecca, eyeing the doorman, wondered why he had addressed her by her last name and had acted so familiarly. Rebecca said to Mandy, "Do you live here?"

A red scarf hung over Mandy's shoulders. She brought it twice around her neck, and said, "I do, yes."

"Oh," said Rebecca, "okay, now I see." But she didn't. Taking her hands to her face, she said, "How long have you been in the building?"

"Fifteen years."

"Hmm. Fifteen years? And did you help my father get an apartment here?"

Mandy placed her hand in front of the elevator door to keep it from closing, and smiled a peculiar smile. She said, "Help your father get an apartment here? You could say that. Oliver called me up about four months ago. He took me for a drink. He said he needed a place. I have the extra apartment upstairs. So I've been letting him stay."

"You've been letting him stay?"

"Yes," Mandy told her. "For now anyway."

"And what do you charge him?"

Mandy began to laugh. "Charge your dad? I would never do that. Especially with his money problems."

Suddenly, Rebecca couldn't breathe. There was a pain in her shoulders.

"Your father is very sweet. It's nice to have him around."

"Right."

"And how've you been, Rebecca?"

"I'm fine."

"You're a lawyer, aren't you?"

But without answering, Rebecca ran from the building. Passing the Morgan, her thoughts were forced into a standstill. Then she began saying to herself, "I'll get away from here. I'll just leave."

She walked faster, faster. Cars were triple parked in front of an office building on Thirty-Seventh, and taxis fought to get through the pack. Rebecca was telling herself that she couldn't just leave New York though. She had work to do. But had Mandy meant it when she'd said she wasn't charging her father rent? She had, hadn't she? Then what had her father been doing with the money she'd been giving him? As if the answer to her question were on her phone, she looked at the device. She had missed three calls from her office. A man on the sidewalk was trying to get her attention. He had on headphones and he was dancing. He passed a glossy, index-sized card into her hand. She gave him a look, like he had violated her. Her skin hot and eyes filling with tears, she began to scream, "Don't touch me!"

But with the headphones on, the man couldn't hear her. Rebecca realized she was standing in the middle of the sidewalk. People were trying to get past. They knocked her one way, then the other. She had to get to the curb. But even that was difficult now, for there was no space for her to move.

XI: REFRIGERATION

Twenty minutes later, Rebecca went to the bank. In the desolate tinker-toy room, the teller accepted Rebecca's withdrawal slip and I.D. and, within a minute, passed an envelope with $7,634.08 back through the window. She went to sit on one of the couches in the waiting area. Soft music piped through speakers embedded in the ceiling. Rebecca took out her phone. But in how many words could she say it? Ten? Maybe fewer.

"I saw Mandy in your lobby. No more money."

That explained it all, did it not?

At the next moment, Rebecca picked up her phone and began to write an email to her father. She spoke of encountering Mandy in his lobby, but also of knowing that he hadn't been paying rent all this time, that he had been lying to her and abusing her generosity. She said that he was cut off, and that he should stay away from her.

"Don't call me. Don't write. Don't show up at my apartment. I don't want to see you."

She wished him well with his lawsuit. Then erased those lines, and said that he had behaved despicably and that she would never forgive him for this—and then sent the email.

A moment later, she thought, *I have to get out of here.* She left the bank and started home in a taxi. The street light at the intersection of Fifty-Seventh and Madison was off. The sun was blocked out by the IBM Building. Two white-gloved police officers blew their whistles, trying to get vehicles to pass. The traffic cop was screaming, "Go! Go! Go! Go! Go! Go! Go!" The driver slapped the steering wheel. He said, "Go where? Where does she think we can go? We've got no room anywhere."

Fifteen minutes, the taxi was pulling up in front of Rebecca's apartment. She asked the doorman not to ring up for any reason. On her doormat, she saw the notice about the increase to her monthly maintenance and left it where it was, pushed open the door, dropped her bag, and started pulling off her clothes, first her jacket, then her top, next her shoes and socks, and finally her pants. The sun was bright in her room. She lowered the shades, crawled into bed, pulled the covers over her, and slept until 5 a.m. the next day.

The moment she woke, her overwrought nerves propelled her from the bed and she went out into the streets at once with her red Peugeot. She felt an instant gratitude for the bicycle. Without it, where would she be? Under the covers being devoured by her mind, in all likelihood. The exertion and the wind and the motion was a good temporary cure. At Fifty-Ninth, she cut over to the West Side Highway and rode downtown, past the Intrepid, and Chelsea Piers, and farther south to Battery Park. The city was so quiet and empty and peaceful. She circled back uptown through the Financial District and Tribeca. Crossing over Canal on Sixth Avenue, she cycled east on Prince and turned onto Wooster Street.

There was her grandparents' loft. A light was on in the art studio. A window was open, too. Rebecca stared in from the sidewalk across the street. Was someone inside? It seemed like it. She could hear a radio coming from there. And now she could see the dark hair and forehead and eyes of Jerome. What was he doing that caused him to move so rapidly from one place to another? More importantly, why was he there at all?

From below the window, she called out his name. He didn't hear. She tried again, to no avail, and decided then to ring the buzzer. Suddenly Jerome was leaning out the window. He was only one story up. However, there wasn't much light on the street, and he couldn't make out Rebecca.

"Jerome, it's me."

"Rebecca?" He disappeared for a moment, and then stepped out through a different window onto a fire escape. Now he was smiling down at her. "What are you doing here?"

"I could ask you the same question."

But Jerome was in a frenzied state, and he made nothing of her comment. He said, "You've got to come up and see this."

Rebecca chained her bike to the scaffolding outside. Jerome buzzed her into the building. The elevator door opened onto the second floor, and Jerome was all of a sudden hurrying her into the art studio. Now he was holding out his hands in the direction of eight old refrigerators. They were white. The shelves of each were stacked with books. Jerome began adjusting the doors. He had a very specific idea of how they should be positioned. His expression was one of intense focus. He said, "Rebecca, I'm so glad you're here. I've been working from Ben's plans. They're amazing, aren't they?"

Rebecca was impressed. She said, "Yes, Jerome." She made a loop of the refrigerators. She examined them from every side. "I think Ben would be very happy about this. You've pulled off something special here."

"Thank you."

Jerome seemed to become full of wanting and hope, and his facial muscles began to work to keep back tears. He went once around the refrigerators, walking off the emotion of it. And then, smiling through his grief, he stood up straight, his head cocked. His elbows pointed out at the sides. He told Rebecca to take a closer look. There were all kinds of books loaded into the refrigerators: encyclopedias, cookbooks, how-to books, fiction and plays and poetry. At the bottom of one refrigerator, the fruit and vegetable bins had been removed to make room for Ben's journals. Taking one in her hand and flipping through the pages, Rebecca examined her grandfather's frantic handwriting, his to-do lists, the way he boxed off important things. There was a sketch of a television with an X through it on one page; he had needed the cable company to come over and fix his connection. Three pill bottles were drawn into a margin on another page; it had been time to refill his medications. There was a lot of arithmetic being done. Ben might have found beauty in the coffee stain, the brown rings were everywhere. Rebecca saw how he had asked himself, on July 11th, 1992, to quit smoking cigars. That same day there'd been a deal on Ocean Spray cranberry juice at the IGA: 32 oz. containers, two for one. She turned the page, to July 12, 1992:

Need eggshells for the next piece. Go to Buffa's and ask for theirs.
Go to Bigelow. New shaving kit.
Bread, chicken, sunflower seeds.
Pay phone bill.
Amaze yourself!

Suddenly she looked at Jerome. Some new discovery had gripped him. He was crossing the studio to a refrigerator. He began re-angling the door. Shifting one refrigerator door meant shifting them all, however, and he did that now. It was difficult for Rebecca to believe that he wasn't simply delusional. Well, what did it matter if he were? Her grandfather's old assistant enjoyed moving these doors around. Why say anything about it?

"These refrigerators will be at MOMA one day," said Jerome. "I'm going to make Ben famous. I mean that."

"I'm sure you do. But how many unknown artists have become famous after death?"

"I don't know. How many?"

"You can count them on one hand."

"If it's happened before, it can happen again."

"What do you even know about any of this business?"

"I know that Ark was a genius."

"Even if it were possible to get Ben's work out there, it would mean dealing with my father and his sisters. You'd be welcoming those mental cases into your life. That's not a problem for you?"

"No."

"Are you aware that they're in the middle of a lawsuit?"

"Yes."

"And you'd poke your head into that mix?"

"Yes."

"And if they said no?"

"I'd do it anyway. He saved my life, do you know that?"

"Saved your life?"

"Yes."

"Jerome, he hired you to work a job which a hundred people had already tried and quit."

"He made me fit for this world. I can do anything now."

"And you want to focus on making Ben famous?

"Who owns the rest of Ark's work?"

"It's not official, but I assume Doris will. The whole estate looks like it'll go to her."

"So set up a meeting with Doris. I have to talk to her about this."

"I won't deal in business matters with my family."

"You won't have to be there."

"Sorry, Jerome."

"Do you believe in Ark's work?"

"Believe what? That it exists?"

"Would you be happy if people came to know about it?"

"I don't care. And being that he's dead, I don't think he would either."

"Please, Rebecca. Talk to them."

"No."

"For all I went through with Ben, please."

"No. I'm sorry. I have to go."

Jerome followed Rebecca to the elevator. He was telling her that he wouldn't give up, he had big plans for Ben, he would put his whole life into the endeavor, he would convince Ben's children that he was the right person for the job, he would organize Ben's catalogue, he would make people aware of his art, get Ben a show, first in New York, and then in the world beyond it. Give him five years. Give him ten. He would do it all.

Rebecca wished him good luck. She was waiting for him to let go of the elevator gate so she could leave. But then, the moment he released the metal handle, she called out to him. She had one more thing to say.

She had to ask a favor of him. Yes, she had to say it: "You were a witness to my grandparents' last will and testament. My father needs you to testify about Eliza's cognizance at the time of her signing. Please, don't ignore him. He'll end up with nothing if you do."

Jerome leaned back from the waist, struck by some idea. He said, "We could help each other, Rebecca."

But Rebecca shook her head, and closed herself inside the elevator, pushing for the ground floor.

One week passed and then another. Rebecca didn't hear from her father. But what of the voice which had been chattering on in her head of late? Had it not reached a crescendo on her way home from work the other day? Had she not almost fainted on the subway platform during rush hour? To Rebecca, an emotional collapse of any kind seemed impossible just a short while ago. But bitterness, and rancor, and an uncertainty in herself had gained so much strength over these past weeks. She woke in the night worrying about whether her father could afford his breakfast. Then, sitting up in the dark, she would call him a hustler, a dirty manipulator. At the next moment, she would beat her chest, revolted by her own callousness. Why, he could make as many mistakes as he liked because he had raised and supported her for twenty-five years. But out on the red Peugeot an hour later, the sky still dark in the small hours of the night, she would think that she should cut him out of her life forever. He had conned her out of so much money. How could their relationship ever recover from that?

Then, that afternoon at 1 p.m., Rebecca knocked on the office door of her colleague Randy Nobel. In the two years since walking out on lunch at the Carnegie Deli, Rebecca had spoken of making it up to him. It had become a kind of running joke for them. Rebecca would apologize. It had happened so long ago, but did he ever think he would forgive her? Could they go back, try again? She would stay the whole time, she promised. Randy would hold his hand at his heart, lower his eyes, and shake his head no.

But today, Rebecca proposed lunch at the Carnegie Deli, and Randy took his brown slouch hat off the door hook and followed her toward the elevators. Every employee in the building seemed to be going to lunch just then; the elevators were packed, and lines of people were backed up at the turnstiles in the lobby. Rebecca checked her pockets for I.D. She would need it to get back into the building. They cabbed to the deli. Last time, Rebecca had taken off before she'd had the opportunity to sample any of the food, and Randy said that if this were a true redo, then they had to keep to their previous order: a Nosh, Nosh Nanette and a Millie's Stuffed Cabbage. But Rebecca couldn't eat or talk or listen, and she wondered in the noisy dining room why she had proposed going out to lunch with Randy in the first place. She observed people devouring foot-high piles of meat stuck between bread, and shriveled salamis hanging above the display case, and a waiter hunkered over a table taking the order of a small child being urged on by her parents, and Randy in his Teddy Roosevelt getup—and she felt herself coming unhinged. She could not trust her own words. To her own ear, they sounded wrong, insincere. Her hands were shaking, her heart pounding. She didn't know if she could stay in her seat in this restaurant just now and not lose it. But she watched Randy finish his meal. Then Rebecca paid with a fifty, and they went out of the deli. She had expected the natural light of day and the fresh air to pull her a step or two back from this vertiginous mental place.

But no.

In a taxi with Randy, Rebecca clutched the strap of the seatbelt crossing her chest and pushed her feet into the floor of the car, doubting that she could hold it together the whole way back. Her fears were exacerbated by a vibration that started up in her tongue and traveled through the roof of her mouth. The sensation weakened when she entered the lobby of the office building. She thanked Randy for joining her. Said she would see him upstairs in a moment, she had to make a phone call. Randy tipped his slouched hat and left.

What happened next was difficult for Rebecca to recall even ten minutes after the fact. A finger began to tap hard against her shoulder, and she turned around: there was her father, in a loose-fitting tweed suit. Perhaps he'd just gone into a public bathroom and doused himself with water. His gray hair was wet and pushed back on his head, and his bearded face, the white hair grown woolish, was damp. His over-exuberant smile was pure unreality, and his eyes projected a sort of "ta-da" expression, as if his appearance were the result of a magic trick. He tried to hug his daughter. But for Rebecca, drawing back from her father was a pure reaction, made without thought or hesitation.

She lowered her head at an angle and circled her jaw in the palm of her hand and listened to the reverberations of sound—the footsteps and voices beneath the two-story-high lobby ceiling—all the while coming in and out of herself.

"...Sheila's back in Los Angeles," Oliver was saying. "But I won't leave New York. This is my city, my home. I'm best here."

Now something shifted in Rebecca, and her awareness moved off her father's voice onto the sound and feeling of her own heartbeat. It was so loud, to her. Too loud.

Oliver was telling her that he was sorry, he had broken a promise and called up Laura and seen her more than once. "But just like you said, she's still in love with me. She wanted to be together every day. I told her we could only be friends. And she couldn't handle it. She had a complete meltdown. We had to go to the emergency room to get her a Valium and I took her home afterward and I told her that we couldn't speak. I'm sorry,

Rebecca. I should have known better. Of course, Laura and I can't be friends!"

Rebecca said, "Dad, what did you do with all the money I gave you?"

Oliver told her he had been paying rent with it and buying "the essentials."

"Dad, I wrote you an email. Did you read it? I ran into Mandy. She said you've been living for free in her extra apartment."

"Free? She was lying to you."

"Dad—"

"This is fucking outrageous. You know she's in love with me, don't you? She thinks just because I live in her apartment that I should have to sleep with her."

"Dad, please."

"I can't be in that place anymore. I have to move, but you ripped away my funds—I don't know why."

Rebecca looked over her shoulder. She touched her head. The blood was leaving it. She said, "You stole from me."

"Stole!"

"Yes, Dad. You stole."

Oliver, bending low, his arms almost sweeping the floor, said, "That's insane, Rebecca."

"It is insane, Dad. But you did."

"Well, I need money." He blurted this out. "You have to give it to me. You can't say no."

His begging horrified her. Who was this man? She said, "I'm sorry, I won't give you any more. Not now."

"Not now!"

"No."

He said, "Well, when? Give me an idea. In a week? A month? Six months?"

"Dad."

"In a year?"

"I don't know."

"Maybe when I'm old and I can't stand and my mind's gone and I'm totally fucking goddamn helpless? Then you'll give me money? Is that what you mean?"

"Maybe, Dad."

Oliver opened his shirt at the neck to let out heat. He said, "You have to give me something, Rebecca!"

"I can't, Dad."

"Yes, you can!" He took a deep breath, heaving. He said, "What do you expect me to do?"

"I don't know."

"How will I eat!"

"I don't know."

"You don't know! What do you mean you don't know? You do know. I need money and you're going to give it to me! I won't leave here without something."

"I'm sorry, Dad."

"I won't. I won't, Rebecca. You're going to give me something. You're my daughter and you have to."

"No," she said. "I'm not going to do it."

"So what, you'll just let me die out here? Is that it?"

Passersby were beginning to stare. Rebecca saw one of the partners at the firm glance in their direction. She took a step back. But Oliver caught her by the arm. He said, "You have to help me, Rebecca. I have nothing."

Rebecca pulled away from him. Her father's nails left scratch marks on her skin. Rebecca searched her purse for her I.D., said goodbye. At ten feet away, at twenty, at thirty, she could still hear her father screaming. She was a terrible daughter. She should know her life was ruined now. Between them, she would suffer worse. Guilt and remorse would follow her everywhere. She shouldn't think there was any way to get out from under it.

"Mark my words: this—this guilt—this is the whole meaning of your life now!"

XII. ESCAPE

The following morning, Rebecca woke with an idea. She wouldn't go to the office today, but instead, fly to Los Angeles, California. There was no vacillation. Her resolve was strong. She booked herself a ticket for that afternoon, and arrived at LAX just after 7 p.m. She had no luggage to wait for at baggage claim. The car rental outside the airport gave her a white convertible, and she was at the Surf and Sands in Malibu by 8:30 p.m. In the hotel lobby, she took brochures for local attractions. She roamed the gaming room. There was a pool table. The paneled walls were painted canary yellow. The smell of mold was strong. Most of the books were supermarket romances. Rebecca took a copy of *Life Magazine* off the shelf, opening to a photo of Elizabeth Taylor, and she heard grains of sand slide between the pages and land on the floor at her feet. The sun was down. She returned to her room with the magazine and fell asleep reading.

The next day, she went out to the beach early and dozed. She ate a bran muffin and rejected a call from her office. She got in the convertible and went a few miles north to see what was there. She sat at too many traffic lights. The car wasn't as perfect as she'd hoped. The radio didn't work and the roof wouldn't open. But while dialing the rental dealer, she stopped herself. Why, she'd left the beach too soon. She had to go back there. What was she doing out here anyway? Fifteen minutes later, she was jogging beside the ocean. She got down to the Santa Monica Pier and then reversed directions, running slowly all the while. She cooled off in the ocean. Lunch was a banana and a cup of coffee, compliments of the hotel. Afterward, she pulled a sunhat over her head and lay down only a short distance from where the tide came in and the sand became an escarpment, and she rested.

Sometime in the early afternoon, she opened her eyes and there was her mother on the back patio of the hotel. Helen Bloch had a way of making an entrance, even on the beaches of California. At the stairs leading down to the beach, she took the hem of her white dress in her hands. Now she brought her feet together and let go of the dress so that she could undo the pin holding up her black hair. It fell past her shoulders.

Rebecca called to her mother. Helen smiled and took up the hem of her dress again. But then only her shoulders rose and her chin circled the air. She stared down at the beach, staying right where she was. Rebecca rose to her feet then and ran to her mother's open arms.

Helen stood back so that she could see her daughter. Her lips peaked like a sail at the middle. She said, "Baby, how are you?"

"Okay, Mom."

"Are you sure? When I got your message, I was so worried."

"Yes," Rebecca said. "I'm okay."

Helen scanned the beach then. She said, "It's gorgeous out here. Smell the air. You don't get air like this in New York."

"No, that's true, Mom." She imagined her mother would appreciate her taking a deep breath, so she did.

"How long are you staying?"

"About five days," Rebecca answered. She wouldn't take the question to mean that her mother wasn't glad to see her.

Helen said, "To just get on a plane and go isn't like you. Whatever your father did, it must've been awful."

"Yes."

Helen took her daughter's hand. She said, "But we won't talk about that now. Come on. Let's go for a walk."

They went half a mile up the beach to another hotel and drank iced coffees out of ribbed plastic cups and eavesdropped on nearby conversations. There was a canopy to sit under here. Helen talked about the sun and its dangers. She hoped Rebecca stayed out of it. Because skin cancer ran in the family, and who wanted to look old anyway? Helen raised her sunglasses. For the first time in years, Rebecca saw her mother's face, the light eyes kind but proud, the nose bringing softness to the strong bones of her cheeks, the cliffed forehead, the round chin and small ears. Helen said, "I'm sixty-four. Would you ever guess that I'm a day over fifty?"

Rebecca smiled. It was the first time her mother had told her her real age. She said, "You look great, Mom."

They went farther down the beach and found a teenager selling margaritas out of a cooler, and Rebecca bought two. The way the clouds were positioned, the sun was shining through at one minute and then gone the next. But Helen had a ten-dollar throwaway umbrella that she referred to as a parasol, and when the sun was out she pulled Rebecca close and protected her beneath it.

"Oh my God," Helen said.

"What is it, Mom?"

Helen brought the umbrella from her right shoulder to the left, and then she began to squeeze her daughter's biceps. This was very impressive. Rebecca was strong. How had she gotten muscles like this?

"Look at my arms," Helen said. "There's nothing I can do about that sonofabitch gravity. Well, what's your secret, darling? Don't make your mother have to beg now."

But before Rebecca could answer, Helen excused herself—she wanted to bum a cigarette and a light from a surfer. Rebecca watched her mother from a distance. Oh, she could really turn it on when she wanted, with the boisterous laugh and generous smile and the many incidental touches delighting this blonde half her age. Coming back up the beach to her daughter, Helen flipped her hair and rolled her eyes. She asked her daughter to hold her cigarette, and then chastised Rebecca for taking a drag. "You don't smoke, do you? Please don't start."

"I don't really smoke, Mom."

"For me it's too late. I look at a cigarette and I want to consume it, mind, body, and soul. You're not bad like me, are you?"

"No, Mom. I could give it up anytime."

"Then do, please."

They started back to the hotel along the beach. The sun wasn't yet low in the sky. Rebecca took her mother's hand. She said, "I might be done with my father."

Helen became very serious all of a sudden. She said, "You have to think about yourself, Rebecca. Because ultimately that's all anyone is doing anyway. So let's stop bullshitting. If you feel like you're being abused by your father, eliminate him. Don't feel bad about it either."

"I don't know. I think I've done it."

And yet Helen was very worked up now. She said, "Even with my daughter..." But then she paused, shaking her head, her mouth opened but ceasing to speak. At last what she said was, "I'm sorry, but a child is only one part of your life. An important part. But it's not as if you have them and your feelings and desires leave you."

"I don't think that, Mom."

"You have to fight for everything you want in this life."

"You know," Rebecca said, ready to abandon the subject, "I've been riding a bicycle these days."

"Well," said her mother, "I knew any daughter of mine had secrets."

"I saw a rental shop across PCH. Maybe we could go for a ride."

"No. I don't think so. No, I'm no good at sports."

"You would like it."

"Please, Rebecca, I don't want to."

"I know you can ride a bike. And you'll find it therapeutic. It's good exercise. There's really no argument against it."

Helen unfolded her sunglasses and slid them back onto her face. "There's always a good argument against anything, dear."

That night, Helen and Rebecca shared the queen bed in the hotel room. But with all her mother's issues regarding space, was it okay to be so close to her? Did it bother her that their stomachs were side by side, touching? That their thighs, their knees and feet were in contact? Or that Rebecca's arm lay over her mother's chest? Helen did not tell her to move it.

Come morning, their bodies had hardly shifted. After a brief argument about the importance of trying new things, Rebecca and Helen rented bicycles and went up the coast. Helen couldn't ride very well, yet she managed. They stopped at a diner up the road and had poached eggs and tomato slices. The middle-aged waiter clearing their plates at the end of their meal asked if they were sisters. Outside, getting back on their bikes, Helen pointed out that a compliment from a waiter in a tipping economy was still better than no compliment at all. And

Rebecca, strapping on her black helmet, said that of course the more time they spent with one another, the more compliments of that nature her mother stood to receive.

"I've got nowhere I've got to be."

"Mom, I'm happy to hear that."

"Let's keep going."

They went as far as the state park before turning back. Helen rode ahead of Rebecca, talking over her shoulder. She couldn't believe it had been fifty years since she'd last ridden a bicycle. To have suffered through a hundred other forms of exercise and to have neglected all this pleasure and tranquility—what was wrong with her? Why had it taken her daughter yelling at her to see? And if Rebecca hadn't come to town, what then? She would have never known the wonders of the bicycle.

However, a quarter mile from the Surf and Sands, Helen lost control of her steering and crashed into a parked car, falling from the bicycle and hitting the road. Rebecca hopped off her seat, kneeling beside Helen, who couldn't speak except to say, "Oh my God, I'm in shock. Oh my God. Oh my God, I'm in shock."

"Mom, are you okay?"

"Oh my God, I'm in shock. Shock!"

Helen was crying. Her knees and elbows were cut up. Rebecca didn't think her fall had been all that bad, but they walked the bikes the rest of the way. Close to the hotel, they went into a market where Helen, in great distress, bought cheese and bread, red wine, cigarettes, and M&M's. Rebecca returned the bicycles to the rental shop, while Helen went back to the hotel to clean herself up. Afterward, they drank wine and stared out at the beach, eating cheese and smoking. When night fell, they lay in the queen bed and watched the television until after one in the morning, then they fell asleep.

Helen woke the next morning sore and gimpy. The sun was glancing off the wall opposite the bed, turning the brown wooden panels red. Chatter from the porch above could be heard in their room. Rebecca apologized to her mother about the accident.

"It's all right," she said.

"But you didn't want to rent the bikes."

"It's okay."

"Let me do something special for you."

"Stop it. I don't want it."

Rebecca went down to the hotel lobby. A continental breakfast was being served. She toasted English muffins and brought coffee and oranges back to the room as well.

Handing her mother a cup of coffee, Rebecca said, "How are you, Mom?"

"The whole thing's in pain," said Helen, drawing a line in the air above her body.

"I'll go to a pharmacy and get you something for it."

"No, darling. It's okay. I don't like to take anything. As much as possible, you have to train the body to deal with problems on its own. Let it learn to overcome its aches and situations, right? Not that I'm happy," her mother said.

Rebecca sat down in a chair next to the bed. "We could go to a spa today."

"No, I have to lie right here."

"Can I do anything for you?"

"Nothing, darling. Nothing at all."

"There's an outdoor shower. I'm going to go use it."

Rebecca left the room. At the end of the building, before the turn for the beach, she passed a shed where chairs and umbrellas were stowed. The outdoor showers were there. Rebecca stood under the water, a metal chain with a ring at the end of it wrapped around the fingers of her right hand. It wasn't enough to keep her eyes tightly shut—she wept hard now.

After the shower, back in the room, she found her mother on the porch, leaning on the railing in a contemplative pose, cigarette smoke twisting over the lip of the wineglass in her hand. When her daughter got close, she pulled her against her side. She said, "To think of everything you're going through, Rebecca. I have to assume you're angry at me, too. It's okay. Don't spare me or anything."

"No, Mom." Rebecca shook her head. "That's not necessary."

"I couldn't take those Arkins. I had to get away from them. Now you understand it yourself," her mother said.

"I do, yes."

"But something happened toward the end of my marriage with your father…something I've never told you about. Ben called one day and asked me to come down to the loft. He said that he and Eliza wanted to talk. It's funny, I can recall how I felt speaking to him on the phone, with Ben saying that we had something to discuss. It made me physically ill. And I lived under that threat for ten years, Rebecca. But, that day, I obliged Ben. The whole way downtown the anxiety was eating at me. I got there, and Ben, like any good dictator, makes you wait an hour until he comes out to deal with you. And all that time I'm breaking down inside, wondering what it's all about and why I've been summoned. When Ben was ready, he stepped out of the studio and he pointed for me to sit in a chair. I asked about Eliza. But he had never meant for her to join us. He didn't need her for this.

"I had seen him get nasty with people. Never me. But I could sense it was about to happen. He got that icy look on his face and suddenly he said, 'What are you doing with your life?

I mean, what are you fucking doing with it?' I can't say I was completely caught off guard by this. Because where your grandfather had been supportive of my work as an actress, he had also told me countless times that I was being irresponsible with my family. He said, 'You've got to give up this whole acting thing. You should start working for *Shout!* You could have a very good job there and make money. You're a mother and a wife and you can't be running around the country, doing a role here, in Timbuktu, and a role there, in Cocksuck, Alabama. You have to get serious about your life.' I said to Ben, 'You want me to just quit? It's the one thing I've ever been passionate about.' His whole face lit up, and he called me a fucking nitwit. He said, 'Indulging your passion is a privilege, not something we do at the expense of our families' well-being. Now stop behaving like a moron who mixes up fantasy and life.'"

"That's terrible, Mom."

"Well, yes. But usually afraid to confront him…his presence a kind of gag for me and so many people, right?…this time I said, 'What about you, Ben? You neglect your family.' And he said to me, 'I slaved for twenty-five years to build myself up from nothing. I had ten million in the bank by the time I was forty. I took care of my family and earned the right to neglect them. What have you done?' I got home that night and I thought, *I've got to get out of here. I have to leave.* I mean, could you imagine me working for *Shout!*"

"I hate to think of anyone working there."

"And was I supposed to give up on my life and go get run around like some dog by Doris and Sondra? Just to say it makes me shake. See, I'm shaking!" Helen held her arms out at the side so that her daughter could get a good look at her. Then all at once Helen noticed that she'd been talking so much her cigarette had gone out, and she flipped the butt over the railing. She said, "Don't be too hard on your father for spending his whole life tied up with these people. It wasn't easy getting away from them. I had to give it everything to accomplish that."

Now Rebecca's phone began to ring. She pointed the device in the direction of the ocean. "I'd throw it in the water, but my office might need me."

"Who's after you now?" said Helen.

Rebecca read the caller's name. "That's odd. It's Julia Raines."

Helen crossed her arms and angled her head. She said, "I don't think I've seen her for thirty years. She had a Japanese husband, I remember. He could make wonderful sushi. Your dad and I would go to their apartment and all night we would drink sake and he'd make such great food. This was back in the '70s, before you had so many Japanese restaurants in New York and everywhere else, and you hardly ever ate it."

"I wonder why she's trying to reach me," Rebecca said. "It's disconcerting. The last time she called, it was to say that my grandfather was dead. She doesn't mind giving bad news. She seems to like doing it. You think my father's okay?"

"Rebecca, yes, your father is fine. Here's your chance. Stop this. Take control."

Rebecca said, "I know, you're right." But at the next moment, Jerome was calling. And Rebecca immediately tossed the phone over the railing. They watched it fall into a bush below.

"That must have cost five hundred dollars."

"I don't care," said Rebecca. "I spent fifteen hundred on the last-minute ticket here, and I'm throwing that money away by being at the mercy of that thing."

"All right," Helen said.

Rebecca frowned. "I'm just sorry you've hurt yourself. Let's go swim in the ocean. It'll help your cuts heal."

They changed into bikinis. On their way to the beach, they stopped in the hotel lobby to have a cup of coffee and a banana. The hotel proprietors, old and married, stood behind the wicker desk, their tanned, liver-spotted faces peering out from beneath wide-brimmed straw hats.

"How's it going?" they said, in unison.

"Oh, doing just fine," Helen answered.

"Tell us if we can do anything for you."

"Thank you," Rebecca said.

Out on the beach, Helen began to ask why two people who didn't care for hospitality would go into the hotel business. "I mean, did you see how they were looking at us? Like they wanted us to get lost."

"I didn't get that feeling, Mom."

"Then what were they staring at?"

"I'm not sure."

"Really, it makes a person want to get the hell out of here," Helen said. She pushed her sunglasses up on her face, reclining back onto her towel.

Rebecca lay down too. She thought of her phone now. Was she going to abandon it? But here at the beach, with her mother, the ocean, a warm sun, the phone would continue to interfere. Of course, her office would want to be able to contact her. Moreover, her mother wouldn't stay forever, and then Rebecca would like to drive up the coast, to Big Sur, to San Francisco. To not know her way on any road or street—no, she'd want the phone for the next part of her trip. She should get it. She'd have a use for it.

"I'll be back in a second."

A moment later, Rebecca was down below the hotel room's cantilevered porch, kneeling on the edge of the manicured loop. She reached in through the lower part of the bush. Her knees hurt against the rough stone ground. She couldn't find the phone. Had someone found and taken it? Or had it fallen into another bush? But she'd seen it go straight in through this very one. She searched through an adjacent bush. She walked her fingers through twigs that poked at her hand. A leaf slid partway underneath her fingernail, touching off a sensitive nerve. And then there it was, the phone, between the coiled branches. To have it back in her hand brought on a feeling of intense joy. Then she looked:

Nine missed calls.

Jerome twice, Julia Raines once, her stepmother three times, Laura, the office, and then a New York number she didn't recognize. She hurried straight back onto the beach, to her mother. Her legs felt ready to give out. She held out the phone for Helen to see. "Mom, they're calling me. All of them."

Helen was curled up on a white towel. A bottle of white wine sweated in the crook of her arm. She lifted her sunglasses, staring disappointedly at her daughter. "I thought you were done with that thing?"

"No," said Rebecca.

"So what, then?"

Rebecca kicked at the sand, her balance uneven. "What should I do?"

"You can go and be a part of their ball, or not. It's up to you. But you can't have it both ways." Her mother sighed. "Maybe you want to think about how these people add to your life. What are they offering? What do you get from knowing them?"

Rebecca took the bottle of wine from her mother's hand, drinking. She got sand on her lips. "I don't know."

"What do you mean?" her mother said, angrily.

"I mean that I don't know." She tugged at her earlobe. "It's hard, Mom. I'm not sure if I can eliminate people the way you can."

Helen said, "You have to practice at it. I already told you it doesn't come easy."

"I know. I know," Rebecca said. "But I'm not sure if it's for me."

"Well," Helen told her, "you don't have to start now. There's another option. You can get bullied by them for another week or month or year or decade, and then decide."

"Mom, please." There was a tube of sunblock at her feet. Rebecca exchanged it for the wine bottle, took a dot of the white cream onto her fingers, and began to rub it into her skin. She said, "Give me a chance. I'm still figuring this out."

"You have to really want it," said Helen.

"I think I do."

"You'll need more than to just think you do."

Rebecca said, "Okay, thank you, Mom. That's enough for now."

"You're probably just not ready."

"No," said Rebecca. "Maybe I'm not."

And she went to swim in the ocean.

But what was her mother doing, personalizing her struggle like this? Was her conscience bothering her? Yes, to see her daughter have to fight this way, she couldn't help but feel responsible. She dove beneath a wave and came up for air. Wiping her eyes, she thought she saw in the far distance a whale discharge water through its blowhole. She waited for the whale to shoot up water again. But then there was nothing more to see out there toward the horizon. She went under another wave. And coming up, she thought, *But was it a whale I saw?* Again, she looked out as far as her eyes could see. Now another wave came over her, and then another, and she concluded that her eyes had made up this whale. She returned to shore and her towel. She felt shaky. Helen suddenly stood. There was a frantic, suspenseful air to the manner in which she looked around herself on all sides. Her mother said, "I'm sorry, darling, but I have to get back to work. I have to go home. I have to speak with my people."

"Okay, Mom."

"We can have dinner later. You can come to my place."

"Okay."

"Good. I just, I have to go."

"Well, let me help you."

The women began to pack up their beach things. They didn't look at each other. They walked up from the beach to the hotel's back patio, like a series of putting greens separated by curving brick walkways. There were no guests anywhere. Helen had brought only a bikini and a dress in a shoulder bag. She asked Rebecca what time she would like to come over.

"I might start driving up the coast soon. I'll have to see if I haven't left town. I did rent this car, after all. I should use it."

Helen brought her hands together behind her back. Her hips came forward, as if to temper some unwanted feeling. She said, "You'll let me know."

They hugged goodbye. Rebecca remained at the open door of the hotel room until her mother was out of view. Then she went and closed the shades. She could still hear the ocean. A warm breeze blew in through the sliding patio doors. The light passing the curtains was orange. On the bed, Rebecca sat against a stack of pillows with her legs straight and crossed at the ankles. Her hand groping in the air beside the bed, her fingers folded around the lip of a wine bottle. She turned on the television and drank. She was pulled in by a film about a young American man and woman studying at the Sorbonne, their relationship started on long walks in the Bois, café nights and conversations on art. But Rebecca fell asleep. She didn't wake until night. Suddenly she sat up and cursed. The time was 11 p.m.

She had to call her mother. She reached out toward the bed-side table for her phone, but it wasn't there. She got up and turned on the light. She was disoriented by the unfamiliar feeling of the room. The brown ceiling fan turned slowly above the bed. Rebecca saw her phone on a chair next to the door. She stared at it for a long while and then got back under the covers. It was all right. She didn't need to call her mother. Had Helen even thought that they were actually going to eat with each other? Had she wanted her daughter to come over? No, Rebecca didn't think so. The covers were soft against her skin, the sheets warm and the ocean sounding a luxurious phrase. What of getting in the car and driving north now? Beginning the journey? Going?

Or perhaps a simple beach walk instead. She looked out toward the patio, the curtains moving with the wind. The bed was holding her with a perfect sort of affection. On the television, the same Americans-in-Paris film was being replayed. Rebecca only had to rewatch a few scenes and she would be back to where she'd left off last time. She was excited to watch now. But, once again, in only minutes, she fell right asleep.

The following morning, she woke with a strong hunger. It was 5 a.m. Restaurants weren't open yet. She fished out a bag of peanuts and a cereal bar from the minibar and made coffee on the machine in the bathroom, mixing in the dehydrated milk and leaving the red straw in the Styrofoam cup. She put on the television. Again, she thought of calling her mother. Or getting on the road. The covers and sheets were tangled up in a pile to the right of her. She stuck her feet beneath it and watched a Masterpiece Theatre production of *Little Women*. Every few minutes, she checked the clock to see if it was time for breakfast in the lobby. She was famished. Eventually, at 7 a.m., she went downstairs and put some of everything on a tray: two hardboiled eggs, a bowl of cornflakes, plain yogurt, an English muffin, a glass of orange juice, an apple. Climbing the stairs leading up to the second floor, the tread creaking under foot, she reminded herself to be careful not to spill.

Then Rebecca heard her name called. She turned and saw one of the hotel proprietors, the old woman, with her large-brimmed hat pulled low. Rebecca thought she might be doing something wrong. Taking too much food, for instance. Or was she not allowed to bring breakfast back to the room? There were tables to dine at in the lobby. Silverware was already set on napkins. Milk for coffee was arranged there. But Rebecca wanted to eat in bed, in front of the television. She said, "Good morning," and smiled.

The woman didn't smile back. Her mother was right. There was something inhospitable about this person. "Rebecca Arkin," she said, "you have a message from your secretary. She says to call her."

Up in her room, Rebecca dialed work. Leaning in the doorway of the bathroom, she faulted herself for ever giving her office the name and number of the hotel. It was a quarter after ten in New York, but her secretary still had the sound of sleep to her voice.

"Rebecca," she said, "you have messages."

"Yes. Do you want to tell me?"

"Your father, and a woman named Sheila, and someone named Jerome."

Rebecca ambled over to the bed and sat. The tray of food was on a chair in front of her. She began squeezing the English muffin, forming a small puddle of butter on the plate. Although her secretary was still speaking, Rebecca said, "Thank you," and hung up. She thought of the rental car. *I should take off up the coast this minute.* But instead she got in the bed and ate breakfast. She slept, and woke at 2 p.m., and eyed the television and then the window, visualizing the beach and the ocean. However, she had the thought, *No, that's okay. This is good. I'm fine right here*, and her head fell back against the pillow, and she was soon asleep again.

Rebecca spent the next two days in her hotel room. She didn't step foot on the beach. Sleeping late each morning, straight through breakfast, she had food from local restaurants delivered to her room and left the metal takeout containers pooling with sauce everywhere. White boxes with handles like paperclips were stacked one atop the other next to the front door. Chopsticks and plastic utensils were lost in the bed. Over the past thirteen years, Rebecca had been too busy at law school and then at her job to watch television. Now she took in program after program with intense interest. Her eyes burned, her minibar was empty, her scalp itched, her skin was peeling. The hotel proprietor telephoned the room at one point and Rebecca was startled when the phone rang. She wanted to know if Rebecca was planning on paying with the credit card she had put on file.

"Yes," Rebecca told her. "You can run it. I'm not sure how many more days I'll be staying. I'm not leaving today."

In fact, Rebecca spent an additional week at the Surf and Sands. She let housekeeping come in one afternoon and change her sheets and give her more toilet paper and clean towels. Meanwhile, Rebecca went to the beach. She put her feet in the water and shut her eyes and wondered if her mother had tried her on the phone. Or called the front desk to find out if she'd checked out. The incoming ocean rising up to her knees, Rebecca thought, *Well, I hope I haven't insulted her.*

For Rebecca, the cleaned-up hotel room seemed off compared to the one she'd left fifteen minutes before. But over the next three days, she brought back all the mess and disorder, the paper takeout bags, the empty wine bottles turned on their sides along the bed, the smell of sweat and sleep pungent in the air. She kept the doors closed, the shades drawn, the ringer on the phone off. When, she wondered, would she want to leave this room? She gave herself timetables. Tomorrow. Or, two days from now. In twelve hours. First a shower and a nap and then off she'd go. But then Rebecca considered that she was here, at the Surf and Sands, and what was the likelihood of her ever returning? *I should take advantage and rest and be out of reach from all people*, she said to herself. She put on the television and shifted back into the pillows. She said, "This is bliss. This is really wonderful. I am happy for the first time in years."

EPILOGUE: MESSAGES

When Rebecca checked out of the Surf and Sands, she got into her car and began driving north.

"...Because I've tried to live normally. I tried with your dad. But we couldn't make it work. His family dominated him. Now look at everything that's happening. Did I not predict this? Did I not try to get him out? I did—I tried so hard, Rebecca. I'm sorry that you've had to deal with all of this. It's not right. These people are sick. But I don't know how close I can get to your dad now. I'm not sure if it's good for me. You remember how much help I needed after he left me. I'm doing as much for him as I can, though. I rented him a new apartment near me. I've given him money. But he's telling me you won't talk to him. Rebecca, don't do that. Call your dad. He loves you. He loves you more than anyone. Don't hurt him. Ciao."

She didn't know where she was going. But she wasn't returning to New York City.

"Sheila here. Your dad's not doing so hot. Have you guys spoken? He and I talked two days ago, and he didn't sound like himself. Go over and see him. Thanks."

She was after reinvention now, a new life, and she didn't know how to make that happen back home in New York. Was it even possible? She wasn't sure it was. Maybe for someone else. Someone who really wanted to fight that battle, and to win it. She didn't have that desire.

"Rebecca, it's Jerome. Call your aunt for me, please."

She sold her apartment and settled in Memphis.

"Rebecca, it's Sondra. I'm calling to say hello and to let you know that, with everything that's going on in the family, I am still your aunt and I still care about you. I would love for you to come spend a night or two up at the house in Scarsdale. It's very beautiful here, and I know your cousin would love to see you. It's a shame that no one in the family is talking. But especially with my parents gone, we should all be working to try to come back together. Your Uncle Steven feels the same way, and he sends his love to you. Know that I am always here for you. I have your best interests at heart. I remember when you were born. I was there in the hospital. It was a very special day for everyone, and you will always be very special to me. Call me if you like. We love you."

ACKNOWLEDGMENTS

Thank you, Silas and Jenna.

Thanks to my mother and Sepp.

Thank you to Carrie Howland, Guy Intoci, Michael Seidlinger, Steven Seighman, Will Akers, Michelle Dotter, Scott Cheshire, Wayne Kabak, David Burr Gerrard, Philipp Meyer, Spoon, Richard Danielpour, Phillip Blumberg, Mark Fischer, Benjamin Kruger, and Steven Isenberg.